BEWARE THE BUGS!

EDITED BY JAMES & CHERYL MAXEY

WORD BALLOON BOOKS!

BEWARE THE BUGS

Edited by James & Cheryl Maxey
editors@inorbit.com

ISBN: 9798835272235

TABLE OF CONTENTS

For anyone who's ever swallowed a fly...

...or had a fly swallow them.

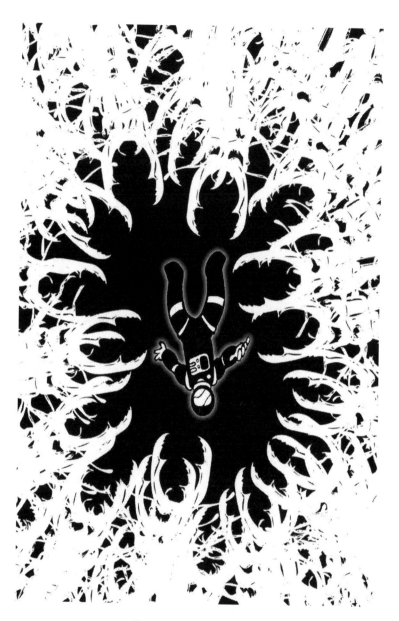

Don't Think, Just Run

DON'T THINK, JUST RUN

DANIEL R. ROBICHAUD

The trees here were different, Zoe Watanabe noticed. Scored with dozens of deep gouges, the sorts of things she associated with pictures from Sol-3. Bears clawing bark out of instinct, the ways cats sharpened their claws on cardboard or scratchers or fence posts. There were no Terran bears, though. Not here on Gamma VI.

Zoe had the protective screen on her helmet raised to allow her a chance to listen to and smell the woodlands. These were beautiful lands, impossibly so. Dangerous, of course, but lovely to the eye, to the ear, to the nose. As she brushed her gloved fingertips along some of these gouged trunks, she caught a whiff of burnt sap. Small black flakes decorated her fingertips when she pulled them away from the bark.

In the war between interest in where she was with the promise of getting back home and trading opinions with her best friends about last night's gossip bombs about this dreamy boy maybe going out with that burnout girl or the nerd patrol's sketchy mischief at the football rally? Well, Zoe was way more interested in going home already.

"Sweetie, I want you to focus on specimen collection, okay?" said Mom. She was a forty-year-old biochemist, trying to instill in her daughter a love for the biological sciences or, if not love, then at least an understanding of them. With her helmet sealed up tight, there was no hearing her but for the tinny sounding comm bud in Zoe's ear. "I don't need to remind you about the dangers—"

"I know, Mom. You drilled them into my head a bunch yesterday."

This time of year was when the basilisk beetles were easiest to awaken. It was all tied to the development of oogu fruit on the fat trunked trees because the beetles' young fed on those fruit as a part of strengthening their mandibular structures.

Mom said, "We are each wearing padded environment suits—"

"Which can stave off singular encounters," Zoe recited, "but they won't let us survive a collapse into a full on nest. Let's face facts, Mom. I know all this stuff already."

The suits were full body suits made from a form fitting protective fabric in brilliant yellow and greens. The material was similar to the stuff woven into riot armors, smart fabrics that assessed impacts and then adjusted fiber angle to repel those impacts. Where military and law enforcement armors were intended to dissuade occasional cartridges from finding and penetrating the delicate bodies beneath, these suits were formulated to repel stingers and natural weapons. They did little to reduce massive concussive impacts, but they stopped small and medium sized penetrations. Dropping into even a modest sized basilisk beetle nest would expose the suits to far too many points of impact, confusing the smart threads and bypassing their protections.

"Sweetie," Mom said, and the condescending tone was too much. Zoe knew that now she was going to get all weepy while trying to bond over shared experiences. Still, Mom tried to sound relevant: "I remember what it was like being fourteen. Curious about the world, yet certain of my knowledge of everything, and unwilling to accept there were some things I didn't know."

As though Mom knew anything about being fourteen anymore, about how the girls in her school could be so awful about being even 1 kilogram over optimal on the weekly weigh ins. As though she had an inkling of how crippling the course work could be as well as being even noticed by someone like dreamy Gads Remmerick ...

"Now, you take this specimen case and find three or four ripe, good sized oogus," Mom said, holding out an oblong box which looked as unwieldy as her brother's tenor saxophone case.

Those cases were the same ones Mom used for field biology classes. All the students there wanted to be in the trees doing the work because they didn't have anything better to do. Mom even bragged that the cases themselves gave her students a concrete reason to think about the work. They were bulky, intrusive and rewarded distraction with pinched fingers and bruised thighs.

Zoe decided not to take it. "I'll carry them. You keep the case."

"Take the case, Zoe," Mom said. "Oogus are delicate and—"

"And I don't need it, okay?"

"Do we need to be pains in each other's necks bright and early on a Saturday morning?" Mom asked. "Will you take this—?"

When Zoe shoved the case right back, it fell out of Mom's grip and tumbled along the forest floor for a couple of meters.

"Nice, Zoe. I hope the storage vessels aren't ruptured."

"I'm sorry, Mom," Zoe wanted to say. Instead, she mumbled the apology. It was hard to talk to Mom, these days. They might be together in a room or right here in the Woodlands, but in many ways they might as well be on completely different planets.

Mom trudged over, delivering a sermon about the importance of respecting delicate instruments, and she seemed completely unaware of the way the ground trembled under her boots. By the time Zoe understood what that meant and called, "Mom, wait!" it was already too late. Mom's boots punched through the thin surface over a basilisk beetle nest.

In an instant, Mom was all but gone, dropped into the ground. Her arms went wide, hands catching roots and harder turf. She stopped plummeting with her head, arms and shoulders up out of that hole, gasping and struggling and … stuck. *Oh no! She was stuck in a basilisk beetle nest!*

"Zoe," Mom said. "Don't! Don't come any closer."

Zoe had not realized she was walking over until that barked order. She wanted to help her mom out of the hole, of course. Pull her up. Mom was right to stop her, though. The ground could be a fragile shell over there.

"Mom, I don't know what to do."

"Zoe, sweetie. Let's find our calm."

"You're in a nest, right? Are they biting you? Are you gonna—"

"Stop talking, sweetie. It's not a nest. Probably a tunnel between chambers. I'm okay. I need you to get back to the Runner. Fetch the tow line. Okay? Can you do that for me?"

"Mom!"

"Don't overthink," Mom said. "Run and get the tow line. Bring it back. We'll get out of here."

"But Mom! I can't—"

4

"Sweetie," Mom said. "I know this is an intense situation. But I don't know how much longer I can hold on. Please move. Now."

At that very moment, the first of the basilisk beetles emerged from the hole, scuttling along Mom's left arm. It was a dozen centimeters long, a larval stage bug. Six legs trotting along with purpose, mandibles testing the suit for flavor.

"Mom!"

"Shh," Mom said. "It won't get me. The suit keeps me safe and my visor is down. You know what you need to do."

Zoe's hand reflexively moved up to slam her own helmet's protective screen down.

Don't think, just run. Don't question, just fetch. Zoe turned back the way they'd come, grateful that Mom used a foliage clearer beam to make a visible path. She'd thought it was a little overkill at the time, of course.

Zoe raced to the path and hurried back the hundred or so meters to where the Range Runner was parked. It was a boxy transport sitting atop six heavy duty terrain crunching tires. Mom kept the rear stowage area packed up with collections gear, environment suits, first aid kits and survival packs. A few centimeters above the midpoint of the front bumper was the tow spool, a coil of high-impact test line perfect for getting a mired Runner back on the trail or for allowing the Range Runner to unmire other vehicles—or in this case, people.

She hit the release switch, and the spool turned freely, making dull clicks that were audible even with Zoe's helmet in the sealed position. She opened the cache for the winch's remote control, dragged the hand unit off its charger, and tucked it into her environment suit's left breast pocket. She tugged on the tow line and it unspooled with ease. She turned back the way she'd come, and gasped. Mom was gone.

Only after wasting a minute craning her neck did she realize that Mom was not gone, but her position was low enough that a few of the colorful, spiky emerald spade plants were blocking her line of sight. What Zoe had been staring at was another hole opened up in the ground, not far off from Mom's position. That hole was much more active, with lethargic larvae spilling out in search of the stinky sweet, overripe oogus.

Something much larger moved in that hole, as well. It was a full sized adult basilisk beetle, and it was rousing from its torpid state. *A nest.*

Zoe wanted to run back to mom, but the tremors of her feet impacting the soil had probably already triggered that nest into action. A slow and arrhythmic walk was the key to getting back safe and getting Mom out of her predicament.

It was not easy, battling the instinct to hurry. Especially when that second hole was visibly widening in Zoe's periphery. A leg poked up from the darkness below, a meter from tip to joint, the remaining two joints as yet unseen. This was not merely an adult; it was a big adult. Basilisk beetles could grow as long as three meters, and their legs spanned another three or so meters, making them huge. The idea that such tiny larvae could eventually grow to such proportions was kind of amazing. Frightening, yet wonderful. Nature offered surprises in abundance.

Her head filled with pleading, prayers to whoever was listening, that she could get her mom out before the Basilisk decided to poke its head out and catch their attention with its fascinators. If that happened, then it was all over.

Zoe tripped twice, and her chest was aching with the need to vent some serious emotions, but she shoved the need to wail or weep aside. There were things to do before she could indulge that luxury. Mom needed her.

A second leg poked up from that other hole, stretching as its owner decided whether or not waking up was worth the effort. The oogus were not as fragrant as they would be during full on emergence season, and the day's temperatures weren't as warm as they would be. Still, Zoe tried to keep her footfalls as irregular as the opening raindrops of a summer shower.

Finally, Zoe reached her mother. The larva that had been crawling on her mom's arm was still present, now accompanied by another. The larvae's mandibles made rasping sounds as they tried to bite her mother's visor. There was no way for her to simply walk and hand the tow line over. "I have to throw this to you, Mom."

"I know, sweetie."

"But I'm terrible at throwing."

"Do what you can, okay? We don't need accuracy. We need you to get close."

Zoe tested the line, whipping it around in a few gentle circles. Then, she said, "Ready, Mom?"

"Go for it."

Zoe tossed the line out. It was heavier than she expected, and it hit the ground earlier than she'd wanted. The weighted clip at the end dug into the earth half a meter away from Mom's outstretched hand.

"Reel in," Mom said, the strain of holding herself in place audible, now. "Try again."

"Mom—"

"I'm slipping, sweetie. " Mom caught a fresh handhold of roots, but they slithered out of the soil like snakes. "Hurry."

Zoe clapped her mouth shut and went to work. She pulled the line, watching the heavy end jitter and bump along the ground until it was in hand. Then, she swung the line over her head like a lasso and then let it fly. The weighted end sailed high, right over to Mom. It was going to be a bullseye. Zoe's breath fairly boiled in her lungs.

Then, everything went sour. The weighted clamp slammed into her mother's helmet, fracturing the face shield. Mom let out a squawk of surprise and lost what tenuous hold she had. Her arms flew up, remaining visible for a fraction of a second, before gravity yanked her out of sight, down into that terrible hole.

"Mom!"

Comm feedback loud enough to make the ears bleed was the only response.

Zoe screamed her mother's name three more times, before the feedback gave way, and a weak voice answered, "Sweetie. I'm here."

"Are you okay?"

"I twisted my ankle when I landed," Mom said. "I can't stand. Can't walk."

There was no stopping the tears, now. They poured down Zoe's cheeks, heedless of her need to get things done before the sleeping basilisk beetle decided to rise and shine.

"You need to take the Runner," Mom said. "Get help."

"Mom, I can't."

"You have to, sweetie. I know you know how to drive, sort of. Dad's been overriding the smart controls and letting you try the gears."

"But Mom—"

"No buts. I can't walk. And I can't stay down here. So, don't—"

"You don't understand, Mom. A beetle's waking up! Right over here!"

There was no answer from Mom. Zoe said, "Can you see the tow line?"

"Yes," Mom said. "But I don't—"

"Can you grab hold?"

"Well, yes."

"Can you clip it onto safety clamp one?"

"It's damaged, sweetie."

"The line?"

"My suit."

"Okay," Zoe said. "But try, all right?"

A glance revealed four of the six legs were moving, probing the surface. A host of larvae were also over there, tasting everything they could reach. There was no time to dilly dally.

"Sweetie, whatever you're thinking … I don't know if it will work, okay? When I fell, I banged the chest plate hard. A good tug might rip the clip mount free. Then, I'll have a hole right over my heart. The larvae will crawl in, and I won't have much time to warn you away. Not that you'd listen. And if the basilisk's roused by then, you'll be in even greater—"

"Please don't give up, Mom."

"I'm not giving up," Mom said. "I'm just facing the facts."

These were facts Zoe did not want to hear, see or acknowledge. She closed her eyes, recalling what Mom said earlier. "I know what it's like to be certain of everything and unwilling to accept there are some things I don't know. So have a little faith, huh?"

Mom was quiet, then. Maybe from pain or maybe from the surprise of hearing her own words parroted by her weepy daughter.

"Clip secured," Mom said.

Zoe fished out the remote control from her suit's breast pocket and hit the blue retract button. The winch on the Runner whirred, as it reeled in the steel tow line. The cabling dug a hard line through the soft shell over the rest of the tunnel and then Mom let out a whuff as it pulled her up the wall. The plate and clip remained secure.

Mom came out of the subterranean level, arms moving in crazy pinwheeling motions, losing a quintet of larvae like a dog shaking water out of its coat after a bath. Her fast moving hands carried her up and along the wall and then onto the surface ground. Even when she'd surfaced, the winch was not finished. It reeled her toward the Runner, dragging Mom along the trail she'd cleared.

Zoe's grin of triumph froze when she saw the adult basilisk beetle pushing itself out of the ground, now. Its legs finished probing the terrain, and the groaning winch must have offered quite the temptation to look around. Zoe watched her Mom get to the truck and hit the red STOP button to kill the winch. It was too late to urge the beetle back to sleep, but at least Mom was back at safety.

Zoe herself, however, was in direst danger.

There was no sense in walking arrhythmically, now. The beetle was alert, eager for prey. Basilisk beetles were omnivorous bugs, as content with rotten foliage as with a warm, savory meal. Those terrible mandibles clacked shut and spread wide, as though sampling Zoe's flavors from afar.

Zoe ran toward the Runner as though her feet were on fire.

The basilisk beetle had already spied her, and it now pounced from its position. The creature had no useful wings to speak of, though a pair of vestigial growths on its back droned mechanically when the insects got excited. Instead, it was a jumping bug, and this one did a fine job bounding off no less than three trees—the blade shaped feet on its six powerful limbs leaving fresh scars on the trunks—before it crashed into the weeds not a meter ahead of its prey.

This specimen was bigger than any Zoe had seen up close and personal. Its hide was a mottled brown color, dotted with bursts of black. From mandibles to thorax tip, the creature measured a little over three meters, almost twice as long as she was tall. Its head was a terrifying horned thing, its black on black eyes nevertheless beholding her. However, it was a twitching set of auxiliary antennae that caught her attention. Though she told herself not to look, Zoe could not help but do so. The movement was enough to draw her attention and that spelled her doom. The antennae had a shimmering quality that fascinated prey animals, human included. It prevented them from moving a single muscle. The longer Zoe stared, the more her desire to run flowed away. Why run when there was such a shiny thing to look at?

Before the basilisk beetle could lean in for the bite, the Runner raced forward along the path, slamming into it from behind. The bug bounded in pain and came crashing down a meter away. As soon as it was out of Zoe's line of sight, its fascinators lost their hold on her, and she could run again. Zoe made it into the all-terrain vehicle, and Mom used her good foot to get them away.

They were halfway home before Zoe said, "It's all my fault, isn't it? You being hurt?"

"Well, maybe not *all* your fault. I'm kidding, sweetie. It was an accident! Everyone's okay. Shaken up, but okay."

"I didn't mean for it to happen, Mom."

"I know."

"And I didn't mean to lose your gear, and—"

"I know, sweetie. Let's get home. We can maybe come back in a couple of days, see if we can recover the box."

"Okay, Mom."

"And sweetie?"

"Yeah?"

"You did good back there."

"Huh?"

"Getting me out of that hole. I ... I thought I was stuck for sure."

"Yeah, well ..."

"Just take the compliment, okay?"

"Okay."

"A wise person suggested I should have more faith in my daughter. I'm going to try, okay?"

"Thanks, Mom."

"You bet, sweetie."

Even when they got home again, the promise of gossip was the furthest thing from Zoe Watanabe's mind.

ONE LITTLE HOUSE

LAURENCE RAPHAEL BROTHERS

Jason's foot was poised over a small anthill by the edge of the schoolyard, next to an overgrown lot. If you lost a ball in there it was gone forever, the brambles were that thick.

No! Please!

Jason looked, but he didn't see anyone. He thought about the ants and how angry they'd be if he messed up their work. He almost kicked the hill anyway, but decided it would be mean to do it after thinking twice.

Later, in math class, Mr. Hardy was talking about the slope of a line when someone hit Jason with a spitball. He thought it was Andrew, sitting two rows behind him, but he couldn't be sure. If Jason made a fuss it would be his fault. He spent the rest of class imagining terrible things happening to Andrew and missed hearing a question from the teacher.

"Jason, a word, please." Mr. Hardy spoke as Jason was leaving the classroom. Andrew smirked as he pushed his way past.

"You've been distracted, lately," said Mr. Hardy. "If this keeps up your grades will suffer. Is everything all right?"

Mr. Hardy may have meant well, but he made Jason late for English, so he had to apologize to Ms. Chen. He spent the rest of the class imagining Mr. Hardy catching fire right in the middle of math, but it wasn't very satisfying because Jason knew his teacher was just trying to help.

The next day in the lunchroom, Andrew screamed and threw his brown bag down on the floor. A swarm of big black ants came boiling out. They skittered all over the room. It was a huge commotion, and Andrew had to sit there, red-faced, while a teacher told him off in front of everyone. It took half an hour before things settled down, and everyone had to rush to finish eating in time, but Jason thought it was worth it.

In math, later that day, Jason saw a bright red ant perched on Mr. Hardy's neck. The teacher didn't know it was there, kept talking about how you could tell if lines were intersecting on a graph. The ant stabbed downward with its mandibles; Mr. Hardy cursed and swatted it away. A minute later his face swelled up till his eyes were like slits and he started wheezing. Mr. Hardy was lucky one of the kids had an EpiPen, but even though he quickly recovered he was carted off in an ambulance and math was canceled. Everyone had to return to their homeroom and wait for their next class.

Sitting at his little desk-chair, Jason wondered if it was just a coincidence, and then he felt a tiny tweak on the back of his hand. When he looked he saw a black ant perched there, its antennae twitching slightly. He almost crushed it by reflex, but then he stopped himself, just in time. The ant was a tiny thing, and didn't seem like it could hurt him. Jason thought for a minute about what it might mean. And then he walked out of homeroom, with no one saying a word, and he didn't stop till he got to the anthill by the edge of the schoolyard.

"Messing with Andrew's lunch was great," he said, "but Mr. Hardy's not that bad. He didn't deserve that."

No response. Jason felt strange, standing out there by himself, talking to an ant.

"You *did* bite him, right?"

Still nothing. He bent over to look at the mound. Just a little pile of sand, a few ants doing ordinary ant things.

"Billions of people don't kick anthills every day. What's so special—"

The tiny ant on his hand extended its wings and flew off into the heart of the brambly lot.

Come to me.

After the first scratchy moments the brambles didn't get in his way at all. Jason entered a dark, green space inside the bushes. It was like another world.

Hi.

Suddenly, she was there. A girl with shiny black skin and faceted eyes, and delicate feathery antennae coming out of her head. She looked to be nine or ten, a year or two younger than him.

I'm sorry about your Mr. Hardy. But I wanted to thank you for not destroying my home.

"Your home? That little thing?"

I live in many homes at the same time.

"What?"

I'm an... association. With enough members working together for long enough, I can appear like this. But before that, if even one of my homes is destroyed....

"Oh!" Jason understood now why that anthill was so important.

That one little house with just a hundred dwellers. Kicking it would have been enough to stop me from... emerging. But you didn't. That's why—

"That's why you wanted to thank me."

Yes. I'm sorry if I didn't thank you in a good way. I didn't know Mr. Hardy would get sick.

Jason flushed. "It was probably my fault. For thinking such bad thoughts about him. You couldn't have known. But what will you do next?"

I don't know. I'm new. I guess I'll… live? I have a lot to learn, though. I wonder if you can help me with that? Since you're going to school and everything. I could send an ant with you, maybe? And maybe you could tell me about the world, and about your kind of people?

"That sounds not so bad. I was afraid this would be really creepy. But it's— you're okay."

Creepy? Me? The girl held out her hard, shiny hand and Jason took it. She giggled in his head, and a moment later he laughed with her.

NOAH AND THE TREACHEROUS JOURNEY HOME

MARK COWLING

Noah kicked the back of his mother's seat with all his strength.

"Noah!" yelled Kate Dudley. She turned around and gave her son a glare that roughly translated to *you'd better not do that again or you'll pay for it.*

"It was an accident!" Noah said. It wasn't. "I was just moving my leg."

Noah and his mother had spent the last few minutes in their parked car, somewhere in the middle of the vast SaveMore! parking lot. The radio was on but turned down low. Mrs Dudley searched through her purse for a coupon that may or may not have existed.

"I can't believe what I'm seeing," said the man on the radio.

"It won't take long. I just have to pick up your sister's birthday cake," Mrs Dudley said. "Oh, and I need to get your father some more cream for... you don't want to know. And I've heard there's a special offer on—"

"Mom! I've been at school all day. Can't we just go home?"

"This giant pit has opened up," said the man on the radio, his voice getting higher and higher. *"A vast sinkhole. And... Yes, something is crawling out!"*

"No! I'm only asking for ten minutes," said Mrs. Dudley, losing her patience. "Is that so much to ask?"

"It's never ten minutes!" said Noah. "If Shelley was here, you'd drive straight home."

"Hundreds of them! They're everywhere! Hundreds of— " said the radio man before Mrs. Dudley switched the device off with a jab of her finger.

"Leave your sister out of this. Why do you have to be such a brat?" Mrs. Dudley said, glaring at her son in the rear-view mirror.

"I hate you!" said Noah. "I hate you so much!"

Noah flung open the car door and jumped out. He ran and ran until he was at the far end of the parking lot.

"Get back here now," said Mrs. Dudley, her voice weak from such a distance but still full of venom.

Noah didn't exactly have a plan for what to do next, but he would have to decide soon since rain was coming. The sky above had grown dark and a sudden cool breeze blew around him.

"Noah!" shouted Mrs. Dudley. She no longer seemed angry, more scared.

Noah could see his mother's lips move again but couldn't hear her. Her voice was drowned out by a high-pitched buzz. The breeze had become a gale and he tugged his jacket closed.

His mother was staring at the sky above him. Noah looked up.

A black cloud loomed above. A black cloud of bugs, hundreds and hundreds of enormous bugs, each the size of refrigerators.

A middle-aged man shot past Noah. As the man ran for cover, one of the bugs dropped out of the cloud. The lone bug swooped down and casually plucked the man off the ground. As he was carried away, pinched by two of the insect's branch-like legs, he looked down at Noah.

Noah stared in horror at the man who screamed and screamed until he had been carried too high and too far away to be heard.

He ran faster than he'd ever moved before.

There were about fifty meters between himself and his mother.

All around Noah, the bugs were descending, falling from the sky like rocks. When each bug had identified a target, it would peel off from the group and aim at its prey. He saw several men and women crying out for help as they were carried away into the sky.

Thirty meters.

Noah threw himself to the ground, gravel tearing at his arm. The biggest bug he'd seen yet careened through the space he'd been standing in and smashed into a parked mini-van. The vehicle looked like it had been hit by a wrecking-ball, but the bug just flicked itself right way up and buzzed off.

Twenty meters.

Noah's mother was charging towards him, looking like she'd happily take on all the bugs by herself. He was just seconds away from safety now. Most of the bugs were headed to the store entrance where they could find easy prey. He reached out for his mother, stretching.

Ten meters.

Noah was hit in the back. It felt like he'd been struck by a car, but then his feet grew light. Noah drifted up and up, carried into the air. A red-hot pain spread through his shoulder.

"Noah!" shouted his mother. She jumped, her fingertips brushing his left shoe.

Noah peered up. The bug above him gripped him with just one leg, pinching his shoulder like a vice. He tried to scream, but no noise came out.

His mother grew smaller and smaller beneath him. He watched her run but soon they were away from the parking lot and she was then not even a dot in the distance. In an instant, they zipped over large stores and then housing. His mother was gone.

Noah didn't dare struggle. Even the treetops were now a long way down; he knew he couldn't survive such a drop. He did his best to remember the way back to his mother as they zoomed over more homes and woodland. As he thought about his mom and whether he'd see her again, warm tears dripped down his face.

There was a sudden jolt.

The bug holding him dropped a dozen feet and then veered to the right.

Noah looked up in horror. Above them was a second bug, this one the size of a large car. The bug was so enormous, Noah could feel the vibrations of its blurred wings.

The new bug darted at them again.

Her hands were shaking so badly, it took Kate Dudley three attempts to get her car keys into the ignition. When the engine fired up, she threw the vehicle into reverse. But it was too late. A huge dark-green bug latched on to the back of the car, causing the whole vehicle to shudder forwards.

There was still time for Kate to get out of the car. Maybe she could run for cover. She would be smart to hide and wait for help.

Kate took a deep breath.

"That's it!" said Kate to no one in particular. "I have had ENOUGH!"

She hit the gas.

Her car's engine roared, the wheels spun but then caught traction. The car shot backwards and smashed into a truck in the row behind.

The bug exploded. Its great body ruptured and spewed out an impossible amount of black beetle goo, like someone popping the world's biggest and grossest pimple.

Kate thrust the car into drive, almost yanking off the gear change lever. The wheels spun for a few seconds in the slime but then she shot forwards and headed for the exit.

Turning left onto Woodland, she headed in the direction her son had been carried.

She didn't yet know how, but Kate Dudley was determined to find her son. And she'd take out any butt-ugly bugs that got in her way.

The two bugs fought a fierce mid-air battle. The smaller bug buzzed erratically, left then right, swinging Noah about as he screamed. With a jagged red streak down its back, the larger bug bullied its smaller foe, ramming into it, smashing the smaller insect with all its weight.

Noah slipped.

His whole body jerked with fear as he lurched downwards. Then he stopped just as abruptly. The bug had lost its grip on Noah's shoulder, but his jacket was still hooked onto the claw at the tip of its leg.

Noah swung about, the world spinning around him, as only his jacket spared him from a deadly plunge to the distant land below.

A shudder went through the smaller insect and down to Noah. Above him, he saw the red streak bug had locked onto its prey. It sank dagger-like mandibles into the smooth shell of the other insect.

They began a lethal spiral downwards. All three locked together, spinning down to the world beneath.

Down and down and down.

They were falling far too fast. Beneath them were the roofs of houses, paving stones, tarmac. Hitting a hard surface at such a speed would be too much, even without a ton of beetle smashing into him.

As the ground shot towards them, meters each second, Noah saw one option.

He slipped out of his jacket.

The world was eerily silent as he fell the last few feet. He watched trees and buildings fire up around him and then...

Noah landed perfectly in the middle of a kidney-bean shaped pool with a massive splash.

Pain shot through his body. All the air was pushed out of his lungs. Hitting the water so fast had hurt more than Noah had expected. The ice-cold pool made him gasp, swallowing a gulp of water.

Noah dragged himself out of the pool with the last of his strength. He coughed and coughed until his throat burned and he had spat out all the water.

He knew he had to get to safety. Soon the bugs would come for him.

Still dizzy from the fall, Noah staggered into the house the pool belonged to. The doors were wide-open. The owners must have fled when the insects came.

He collapsed onto a soft sofa. Noah felt like he could lie there forever. Gradually his breathing slowed to normal and strength returned to his aching body. After a while, he even managed to get to his feet. He wandered over to the kitchen.

Noah rooted around in the fridge – he hadn't eaten for hours and was absolutely starving. As he filled his hands with cold-cuts, a carton of orange juice and a packet of strawberries, something moved behind him.

Noah stood totally still, glaring at a jar of pickles. He could see his own reflection in the jar and the reflection of the kitchen behind him. Something was crouched in the doorway, a creature with twitching legs and spindly antennae that flicked about erratically as if they were each conducting a separate orchestra. Blocking the kitchen's one and only exit was a six-foot long cockroach.

The beast jerked forward into the room and Noah's hand shook, sending the jar of pickles tumbling to the ground.

The glass jar smashed on the hard tiles and the cockroach shot out of the room, faster than any Olympic champion could sprint.

Noah spun around frantically – there was no escape. He would have to leave through the same door.

A broom was propped against the counter. Without really thinking, Noah grabbed the broom and charged through the door screaming as loud as he could, holding the broom like a medieval knight would hold a lance.

The cockroach was only just outside the kitchen. As soon as it saw Noah, it scuttled into the far corner of the living room, knocking over a lamp, and flicking up a rug. The creature squeezed itself as far into the corner as it could.

Noah's instincts told him to run. But, for some reason, he watched the cockroach. It remained in the corner, shaking slightly.

When he took a step closer, the great insect shook even more. The beast was terrified. Terrified of him!

He had an idea. Ducking into the kitchen, Noah picked up a packet of marble-like chocolate candies. He crept back into the living room.

"Hey, it's okay," he said. "Here…"

Noah rolled one of the candies. It spun along the hardwood floor and came to a stop next to the creature.

The cockroach investigated this strange new item with caution. Noah could now see the insect had a wound on its rear left side. A large painful looking dent had been left in the creature's shell-like body. He wondered if the creature had been attacked.

Suddenly, the cockroach sucked up the candy, much like a giant-bug-shaped vacuum cleaner. It clearly liked the chocolate since it sniffed around for another.

Noah rolled more candies, one after another. Each time he got a little closer and the cockroach became a little less scared. After the chocolate was all gone, they were only feet away. Like a puppy, the cockroach grew braver, sniffing out its new friend. Soon Noah could place his hand on the smooth shell of the beast – it was warm to the touch and vibrated softly.

"I think I'll call you Chester," said Noah. "If we ever got a dog, I was going to call him Chester. But my Dad doesn't like dogs."

Noah went and got himself and Chester anything tasty he could find. They ate sugary cereal, bananas, bags and bags of chips, big handfuls of hazelnut spread. By the end, he was feeling a little ill. He thought Chester was looking a bit sickly too, although it was kinda hard to tell.

Both exhausted, they soon fell asleep.

Noah was in that comfortable space between sleep and the real world. He tried to ignore an irritating tugging at his sleeve and threw out a lazy arm to swat it away. All he wanted now was more sleep, beautiful sleep.

With a bone-shaking thump, Noah fell to the floor. It took him a while to get his bearings, the bright light hurting his eyes. He had been asleep on the sofa, but now...

An ant the size of a large dog had his pant leg in its jaws and was dragging him towards the open door. Noah thrust his other leg at the creature and caught it square in the face with his boot.

The ant was kicked over and onto its back. With a flick, the ant righted itself and scuttled back to Noah. It again grabbed his leg and jerked him to the door.

Noah looked around. Chester was nowhere to be seen. "Chester!" he shouted.

He tried kicking again with all his might.

This time the ant was knocked back only a couple of feet and then pounced again onto Noah.

Noah tried grabbing the coffee table leg, but the beast was so strong it still pulled him along.

Chester shot out of the kitchen, his six legs a blur. He charged straight at the ant, hitting it like a battering-ram. The ant was knocked to the other side of the room but again got back up and charged at Noah.

Noah managed to scramble to his feet. He had an idea.

Dodging the ant as it sprinted at him, Noah leaped to the far end of the room. Behind him was a storage closet. He flung the door open just as the ant rushed at him. Hopping out of the way like a bullfighter, the ant was sent tumbling into the closet.

Noah slammed the closet door shut.

The ant could be heard slamming its head into the closed door again and again. Already the wood of the door was beginning to buckle – it wouldn't hold for long.

"We have to go, Chester," said Noah. Chester seemed to understand and followed him out into the back yard.

In the back yard were forty or fifty giant ants.

With no time to think, they just ran. Noah and Chester fled into the street out front. He shut the garden gate behind them, but there were even more ants out front. Before the horde of ants saw them, Noah ducked behind a parked car and held Chester down.

Behind them, the ants from the back yard were smashing into the fence and would soon break through.

In front of them, ants were wandering over to investigate the noise.

Chester turned and pushed the back of his hard shell-like body against Noah.

"This is no time to play," said Noah. The ants were now at the other side of the vehicle they were hiding behind, their feelers twitching and probing, picking up his scent.

Chester backed into Noah again. This time Noah understood.

The ants were far too slow. With Noah sitting on his back, Chester darted down the street. Noah had to hold on his all his strength, his fingers turning white with the effort.

They moved at least twice as fast as any of the ants. Any poor ant that did get close enough was pummeled out of the way by Chester. The giant cockroach and his human passenger smashed through ant after ant and left the rest in their dust.

Chester could change direction so swiftly that Noah found himself sliding one way then the next on the smooth shell he had for a seat. They charged down one leafy suburban street after another until all the ants were long gone.

Noah felt like he was flying two feet from the ground. Like his smaller cousins, Chester didn't like being out in the open. This meant he was constantly zipping around obstacles, dodging mailboxes, slaloming around parked cars, jumping on and off curbs. The effect was to leave Noah almost as terrified as he was when fighting off the ant.

It seemed Chester had an unlimited amount of energy. Perhaps, he thought, they would never stop, until—

A car skidded to a halt in front of them. Chester pivoted and was about to zoom off again.

"Stop!" shouted Noah.

He clambered off Chester, his legs shaky and unresponsive. As Noah ran to the car, its door opened. Noah's mother climbed out of the vehicle and they hugged, each wrapping their arms round the other, safe at last.

"I'm sorry I said those things," said Noah.

"What... Oh, I don't care," said his mom. "I'm just glad you're alright AND OH MY GOD IT'S A GIANT FREAKING COCKROACH!"

It took some explaining, but Noah's mother reluctantly agreed to allow Chester into the car. After all, Noah couldn't leave him to be attacked again by bugs or ants or whatever, not after saving his life.

They drove away from the part of town which seemed to have been hit hardest by the insect invasion. Chester curled up on the backseat and Noah and his mother swapped war stories. As they roared along the deserted road, they passed many strange sights.

There was a whole field of giant writhing worms, looking more like an undulating sea. At one intersection, a fifty-meter-long centipede shot through like a runaway train. And then there was the two-story high spider that made his mom scream for a full minute.

"You know," said Noah. "Dad never said anything about a pet giant cockroach."

Small Magics

SMALL MAGICS

ALEX SHVARTSMAN

Windram watched one of his students attempt a blooming spell. The child, small even for a pixie, struggled with magic. His face turned red with the effort and tiny beads of sweat formed on his forehead.

"Yaow can't even get such a simple spell right," said one of the other children.

"I bet his talent will turn out to be as useless as Frostcreak's," chimed in Ceta.

Windram shushed them.

Yaow glanced up at Windram, and the older pixie nodded with encouragement. "You're doing fine, Yaow. Feel the magic, direct it, let it channel through you."

The child closed his eyes and concentrated, and finally the yellow florets atop the dandelion towering above the pixies straightened out and bloomed. Yaow opened his eyes and laughed with delight.

"There you go," said Windram. "See what you can accomplish when you put your mind to it? Well done, well done."

He showered Yaow with praise, because he knew that the child would fail in many of the future lessons. Pixie magic was only as potent as their size, and Yaow was the smallest student in the group.

Ashai's turn came next. She'd matured early and already discovered her talent. She could animate figurines made of clay. Her magic brought them to life for about an hour; their delicate forms danced in sunlight before they slowed down and their flesh softened and turned back into mud. This was a rare and special talent, and Windram made certain to help her practice it. By the time she earned her adult name, she would likely extend her control to keep them going for as long as three or even four hours.

Ashai hadn't had a chance to begin before the group heard the sounds of something big moving through the grass. The grove around them grew silent. A pair of moths startled from their daytime sleep flapped overhead, and a group of aphids grazing nearby scattered in the undergrowth. Windram concentrated on the booming bits of conversation he heard from the distance. "Gnomes!" he said. "Hide!"

The pixies scrambled, finding refuge under the fallen leaves and behind the thickest strands of dewy grass. They cowered, as a group of four gnomes walked single-file through the clearing.

The gnomes were huge and terrifying, each as tall as the dandelion. Holstered at each one's side was a jagged knife, fashioned out of a whole stone, sharpened and serrated by hand. Some of the knives had remnants of a dried coppery substance on the edges of their blades. It might just as easily have been berry juice as pixie blood, but the fear in Windram's gut suggested the latter.

"This way," boomed the lead gnome. "Not much farther." He pointed a gnarled finger southwest.

Windram's heart skipped a beat. The gnome was pointing right toward the pixie settlement. A raiding party! The gnomes hadn't raided the pixies for several generations, but the last attack had been so devastating that it remained firmly etched in their tribal memory.

He could take flight, high above the brutes and faster than their massive legs could carry them. He could deliver the warning, but the pixies at the settlement would hardly have enough time to flee or mount a defense. And his students—many of them weren't yet large enough to fly.

Windram was no hero. His talent was to nurture and grow small things, his calling to take care of the young. He could stay here and do his job. Guide and protect the children, care for the next generation that would have to rebuild after the gnomes had gone. Surely, hiding in order to protect them did not make him a coward?

He thought back to all the other children and mature pixies back at the settlement, season upon season of them, each with a unique talent and personality. Each worth saving.

He inched toward Ashai. "I will distract and lead them away," he whispered. "When they've gone, the largest of you must fly home and deliver the warning. Have them send help to collect the little ones."

He breathed deeply, trying to calm his nerves, and then stepped from behind the protection of the leaf.

"You there," he shouted at the gnomes. "Go back where you came from!"

The gnomes turned, baring their uneven teeth at Windram, each molar as large as his fist.

"Stupid *and* ugly," said Windram. "Nature hasn't been kind to you lot."

The nearest brute grabbed for him, surprisingly fast and nimble for his size.

Windram dashed away, narrowly avoiding capture. He took flight, staying low to the ground and moving slowly enough to give the gnomes reason to pursue him. He cut his escape close as he led them away from the clearing, a stone knife slicing through the air right next to his face, clawing fingers almost closing around him.

Windram didn't dare look back until he was far from the clearing. He led them away for as long as he could, buying precious minutes for the others, his lungs on fire and his heart ready to jump from his chest. When he knew he could no longer maintain the pace, Windram soared to the sky, above the grass and the flowers, high enough to see the vast trunks of trees rising to the clouds.

The gnomes cursed at him and one threw a rock, but it flew wide and landed at the edge of a puddle. Windram gathered his strength and flew home as fast as he could. He felt exposed so high up, mindful of dragonflies and other predators that made flying above grass perilous, but speed was of the essence.

When he reached the settlement, it was covered under a protective shield. The magic of dozens of pixies, working in concert, created a hard-shell translucent hemisphere the color of amber that hovered just above ground. There was barely enough room for an adult pixie to squeeze through underneath, but not enough for anything the size of a gnome. Windram crawled under the shield to join the pixies on the other side.

"Thank you for sending the warning." Frostcreak offered her hand to help Windram get up on his feet.

He nodded. "Is everyone safe?"

"We sent them away in time."

Only a handful of the largest pixies stayed behind, using their magic to maintain the shield. Satisfied for the moment, Windram allowed himself to rest. He reached both hands into a dewdrop and washed his face. The world outside seemed so peaceful, so beautiful as seen through the amber of the shield. But he knew trouble was on its way.

The gnomes showed up soon enough. Three of them stepped through the tangles of grass and approached the shield. The lead gnome cautiously poked at it with his finger. He then made a fist and punched at it, and finally cut at it with his knife. The shield held firm, shimmering slightly whenever it was touched.

The gnome peered inside and snarled at the pixies within.

"We have no quarrel with you," shouted Frostcreak. "Go in peace, and let us be."

The gnomes pounded on the shield, but it wouldn't yield.

"We want your nectar," said the lead gnome. "Give it to us, and we'll leave."

The pixies fermented pollen grains. For them it was nourishment, to sustain themselves during the cold months, but for the gnomes and some of the other creatures it was a powerful intoxicant.

"The nectar is our food, stored for the winter," said Frostcreak. "If you take it, we may starve."

"We're hungry, too," said the gnome. "Let us have it, or we'll find something else to feast upon." He waved his hand, and the fourth gnome stepped from behind the grass, carrying a hemp-twine net over his shoulder. Windram's heart sank when he realized that four of the children from his group were trapped inside. There were three of the smallest pixies who couldn't fly, and Ashai, who must've stayed behind to try and protect them.

The lead gnome rested his hand on the hilt of his stone knife. "They're scrawny, even for your kind, but they'll do for a light snack if you don't let us in."

The pixies inside the shield huddled.

"We must give in," said Springsun. "Children are more precious than the nectar."

"Without the food stores, more than four will perish during the winter," countered Frostcreak.

Windram rested his hand on Frostcreak's shoulder. "Use your talent," he told her.

Frostcreak's eyes widened as she understood his meaning. Her talent was to untangle—be it branches or hair or the intricate knots that held together a net. It was not the most useful talent—like Yaow, she was the target of some unkind jokes back when she was among Windram's students—but in this situation it was nearly perfect.

Frostcreak worked her magic. Windram peered through the amber, trying to see the knots of the gnomes' net loosen, trying to make eye contact with the children. He caught Ashai's eye and mouthed 'flee' but couldn't be certain whether she understood.

A few moments later, the net suddenly burst, and the four pixies tumbled onto the ground behind a startled gnome. They dashed for the shield as fast as they could, with the other gnomes rushing to intercept them. For a moment, it looked as though all four might make it, but then Ceta tripped over a root and sprawled face down on the moist earth.

Yaow, who was a few steps behind, stopped to help him up. Ceta winced and cried out as he tried to put weight on his right leg. It was twisted, or perhaps even broken. He couldn't fly, and now he couldn't run.

The fourth child made it to the shield and rolled under its edge. Ashai was right next to him, but she turned back and saw the others' trouble. She flew back and grabbed hold of Ceta, straining to fly while half-dragging him along. But too much time had been lost, and the gnomes were now positioned between the three of them and the safety of the settlement.

That's when Yaow stopped and closed his eyes, channeling his magic the way Windram had always taught him. His body shook with effort, and suddenly Ashai and Ceta soared high above the gnomes. Yaow's levitation spell, one he never managed to master in training, worked in conjunction with Ashai's own magic to help his two friends fly.

The gnome who initially held the net caught up to Yaow and hit him hard with his fist, knocking the pixie unconscious. Ashai was unable to support Ceta's weight with her own magic, but Yaow's contribution had been enough to get them farther away from the gnomes along the curved surface of the amber shield, and she managed to drag the smaller pixie under its edge before the brutes could catch up to them again.

With the rest of their prey out of their reach, the gnomes gathered around Yaow's unmoving form.

Their leader turned to the pixies.

"Let us have the nectar, or we'll take our frustration out on him."

The pixies looked at each other again.

"They only have one now, instead of four," said Frostcreak.

"If we give in to them, they'll be back, year after year," said Springsun, his voice filled with reluctance. "Many will perish. Is a single life worth more than that?"

"The life of a child is worth everything," said Windram.

"He could have kept running," said Ashai. "He stopped to save Ceta."

"He made his sacrifice willingly," said Frostcreak. "Let it not be for naught."

35

Windram stared at the resolute, grim faces of the others. "I can't," he said. He turned to the gnomes. "Give us an hour to prepare, and let everyone else leave safely. Then I will let you in."

The gnomes grinned in anticipation of the nectar. "Deal. Now, hurry it up."

Frostcreak glared at Windram. "Who put you in charge?"

"I made the right decision because somebody had to. And now, only I will be to blame during the hungry months of the winter." He glanced at the gnomes on the other side of the shield and lowered his voice. "I have a plan, and only an hour to prepare. Whoever is willing to help, come with me."

The group of pixies headed deeper into the settlement, where the gnomes could not see or hear them.

"What you propose is madness," said Frostcreak, after Windram explained his plan. "It will get you killed, and our homes destroyed."

"Perhaps. But Springsun was right earlier—if we give in to the gnomes, they'll keep coming back for as long as any of us are alive to ferment more nectar. We must fight back, and this is the only way I can think of."

"Our talents are all small, peaceful things. We have no predisposition for war."

"I know everyone's talents better than most, having helped nurture several generations of you," said Windram. "Small magics can be combined together to do amazing things, when there is a will. You can flee now, or you can stay and help me prepare. All of you."

In the end, everyone stayed. Even Frostcreak.

An hour later, a subdued group of pixies left their home. Their magic opened a small door in the shield and they stepped through, one by one, and flew up into the air, out of reach of the gnomes.

The gnomes honored their bargain. They had nothing to lose but time; without the pixies there to constantly tend to and reinforce the shield, it would collapse on its own in a matter of hours, and the settlement would be theirs for the taking.

Windram watched as every other pixie had left, the bigger ones helping the young, until only he and Frostcreak remained.

"Give her the child," he told the gnomes.

Frostcreak stepped through and the gnome thrust Yaow's body at her. The child moaned in pain, still dazed from the blow, as Frostcreak quickly examined his body. She nodded to Windram; young Yaow would be all right. After he nodded back, she lifted Yaow into her arms and carried him to safety.

The gnome leader placed his palm on the amber shield. "The nectar. Now."

Windram used his magic to widen the doorway from within, making it large enough for the gnomes to squeeze through. He waited for the entire raiding party to enter the settlement, and then allowed the doorway to collapse.

The last gnome turned around and tested the shield from the inside. "He trapped us!"

"My magic isn't strong enough to hold the doorway open for long," said Windram.

"Don't fret," said the leader of the gnomes. "Without the vermin here to maintain it, this wall will dissipate soon enough. Now, where's that nectar?"

Without another word, Windram headed deeper into the settlement, the gnomes lumbering behind him.

He came to the mud-brick storehouse and pointed at the lever. One of the gnomes pulled it, opening the wooden doors and releasing the swarm of angry wasps.

For a moment, Windram stood there and admired the last hour's labor.

He thought back to all the pixies working together, molding dozens upon dozens of wasp figurines out of mud— as many as they could craft in an hour—and placing them in the storehouse.

He thought back to Ashai using her talent to bringing them temporarily to life, and to Springsun using his talent of inciting emotion to infuse them with as much fury as a pixie could muster.

Here they were now, angry buzzing wasps with sharp, deadly stingers dripping with venom, escaping from their trap. Each insect was as large as Windram's arm, eager to attack any living creature they encountered. In moments, they would swarm him and the gnomes, and sting repeatedly, and keep stinging until the enchantment ran its course and they reverted back to mud. Windram stood no chance, but the wasps were too small to be lethal to the gnomes.

And then Windram smiled as he looked at the faces of his enemies, and he used his talent one last time.

He made small things much, much bigger.

STUMPED

EVAN TONG

I guess you don't want to play Mud Café with me," Claire pouted to her older brother, Max. Max was squatting in the backyard, his hands on his cheeks and his eyes fixed on a thick tree stump. After a few seconds she tapped him on his shoulder and repeated with a raised voice, "I guess you don't want to play Mud Café."

Without breaking his trance, Max finally said in a quiet and reverent voice, "I'm watching these ants. It's weird."

Claire stooped down so she was eye level with the tree stump. There in the center she saw it. Many rows of small twigs were lined next to each other, forming what looked to be a perfect square of sticks, all evenly smooth and with hardly any noticeable imperfections. A small army of ants nibbled away at the sticks, making them smoother and more uniform. "OK I'm going to go play Mud Café" Claire announced, unimpressed. She stomped away loudly.

Max, continuing his stare at the tree stump said, "Have you ever seen this before?"

"Max, I see ants all the time!" Claire jabbed impatiently.

"But it looks like they're building something," he murmured.

The scorching, stale air of the July afternoon lingered on until Max, hot from the sun dotting through the tree leaves onto his face, decided he had seen enough. He joined Claire, who was adding more dirt and water to some old coffee canisters and stirring them vigorously. He added some leaves and bubbles from his personal supply of birthday bubbles, played for a bit longer, and headed inside.

Two days passed without another thought to the ants, when on a Saturday afternoon, Max and his mother went outside to pull weeds while Claire played inside. Gazing at the backyard, Max remembered to check on the ants. As he stepped closer, he stopped in his tracks and blinked. There, on top of the square of nibbled sticks, were smooth green leaves stretched tightly over the sticks so it looked like one shiny green coaster. He saw piles of sticks, rocks, and even small pieces of metal scattered around the tree stump. The metal that holds an eraser to a pencil, a thumb tack, and various scraps had been dragged whatever immense distance they came from to arrive at the base of the tree stump.

Max's mom was on her knees and pulling with some difficulty on a small root on the side of the house. She didn't look up when Max approached and asked, "Mommy, is it normal for ants to build stuff?"

"What do you think, buddy?" she grunted as the root came loose.

"They build hills and tunnels. But do they build other stuff?" he ventured, feeling a little silly.

"Well, what kind of stuff?" his mother asked as she dutifully began picking at other smaller weeds.

"Like, piles of sticks and stuff?" he asked as he felt like this wasn't going anywhere.

"Sure, they carry sticks and all kinds of things," she responded and then looking up asked "Can you get me the orange bucket in the garage?"

Max opened the back door and called in "Claire, do you want to see something?"

"What?" he heard her call from inside.

"The ants. They're building something," he ventured.

"No thanks" came a short response. Max closed the door, unsure of what he was witnessing.

Max went into the garage and looked around. He found an old toolbox with various trinkets. He picked out some small nails, a few washers, and grabbed a pair of scissors. He found a water bottle in the recycling bin and cut a few odd shaped pieces. He walked cautiously to the tree stump, looking around even though he knew nobody was looking. He carefully shook the various materials onto the corner of the tree stump, then dusted off his hands. He stepped back and squatted down. In no time, a group of ants marched over to the materials, formed a circle, and began walking around and through everything in an organized fashion, their tiny antennae probing in every direction. They reminded Max of tiny dogs sniffing around at a pile of food before devouring it hungrily.

He squatted there for several minutes, watching eagerly to see if anything would happen, but the ants continued their probing without losing an ounce of excitement. "OK Bud, I'm going inside!" called his mother.

"Can I keep playing?" Max asked.

"It's hot and you still haven't brushed your teeth yet," she called back. Deflated, Max went inside.

Later that evening, as the family was ready to go outside for a walk, he raced to get his shoes on and strode quickly to see if any of his materials had been taken by the ants for whatever they were building. To his disappointment, there was only a small fraction of ants on the stump. He looked around hastily and saw a long line of ants slowly making their way towards the rain barrel that constantly dripped a small puddle of water at the back of the house. "You're thirsty...." Max whispered, then looked around quickly, realizing he had just caught himself talking to ants.

"Bud, where are you?" called his dad from the front of the house."

"One second!" Max answered. He looked around and quickly spotted a large, waxy green leaf by his feet. He stooped down to pick it up, turned it around by its stem, then nodded, satisfied with his find. He raced to the rain barrel, opened its spigot, and filled the leaf with several splashes of rainwater. He walked it back carefully to the stump and set it down by its base, then raced to join his family at the front of the house.

"Can we play outside?" Max asked casually when they all returned from their walk.

"Go for it," said his dad as the adults rearranged all the scattered shoes in their garage. Max ran to the stump and stopped, as a large grin grew on his face. There, by the base of the stump, was a large group of ants drinking hungrily from the leaf water. As he drew his eyes upwards, his mouth fell open. There, on top of what the ants were building, was one of the larger pieces of plastic Max had supplied them from the water bottle. It was standing vertical, so the longest part was standing straight in the air, while a group of ants looked to be holding it up by the corners and another group nibbled at the coarse bottom edge.

Max walked over to Claire, who was gathering flower petals for Mud Café. "Oh Claaaaiirre, want to see something interesting?" he prodded.

"It's not those ants, is it?" she responded lazily.

"Claire, you need to see this," he insisted.

"Fine," she said.

Their dad, knocking the dirt from two shoe bottoms, smiled at them. "What are you kids up to?" he asked.

"Max is showing me his ants. He's obsessed," Claire drawled with rolling eyes. Max, with a look of terror on his face, said nothing but tried hard to suppress his rage.

"Ants? Yeah, they make some crazy big mounds this time of year. Is it near our house? If so I have some spray I could get them with," their dad said without any real conviction.

"No, it's far away from the house," Max quickly blurted out, then quickened his pace towards the back of the house.

"See??" He pointed as they got close.

"How did they get that plastic?" She asked with a slight hint of interest.

"I cut it out for them," he said proudly.

"Max, I don't think you should be putting trash in the backyard. Mommy and Daddy wouldn't like it," Claire chided.

"Claire, it's not just trash. They're building something."

"OK, Max," she said patronizingly and walked back to Mud Café.

The days went by and the hot sun dried the dirt so that it felt so brittle it cast a trail of dust from the slightest movement. Max kept an eager watch on his new science adventure and was delighted to see that the tall plastic sheet was now curved into a near cylinder. He had cut some similar sized pieces from a water bottle and laid a variety of other supplies by the base on the trunk. He diligently filled the leaf with water each day for the ants, but by now the leaf was dried out and he was using the bottom of a water bottle as a more sturdy option. The plastic pieces were sealed together by some type of resin; either ant saliva or some type of tree sap. They had even taken some of the metal bits he had provided and secured them at the base of the plastic structure. Whatever they were building, it seemed like it was purposefully taking form.

Finally, he felt like the ant's project had progressed to a point that it was impossible for anyone to say it was normal ant behavior.

"Claire," he said to his sister with twinkling eyes. "You need to see the ants again. It's the last time I'll ask."

She turned to look at him. Without another word, she put down her Mud Café mixing stick and began walking towards the backyard. When she got close, she circled around the whole stump. There, in the middle, she saw the structure. A perfect square of sticks, with leaves wrapped around. They were once fresh green leaves but now they were getting brown and dried out. She saw four washers, with little bits of tin foil wrapped around them so they were connected. Sitting on top of the foil was a small cylinder of plastic: four pieces cut to the exact same shape and glued together with some type of brown substance.

"Did you do this?" she asked with no hint of emotion in her voice.

"I gave them some of the stuff, but I didn't do any of it," Max said solemnly, his brown eyes unblinking.

"Pinky promise," Claire said, extending her hand. Max grabbed her pinky with his and gave one firm shake of his wrist. "What do you think they're building?" she asked, her eyes returning to the stump.

"What do you think it is?" he asked. "It looks like something to me, but it can't be right."

Claire eyed it closely again. "It looks like a rocket."

Max didn't say anything, and slowly nodded his head.

"Why aren't they doing anything?" Claire asked. Max looked back to the stump, then realized for the first time that the ants were hardly anywhere to be seen. The few that remained were lazily pacing around the bottom of the stump. "Do you think they're tired and hungry?" she asked.

"Maybe. I've been getting them water but not food," Max said thoughtfully.

"What do ants eat?" Claire asked.

"Sugar, I think." Max said, his eyes brightening.

They both went to their mother and asked, with only a hint of mischief, "Can we use some sugar for a science experiment?"

Their mother looked at them disapprovingly. "Sugar attracts ants and other insects. You'll have to think of something else for your experiment."

Later that evening, the kids made a plan, finishing their vegetables and dinner as quickly as they'd ever done. "Dessert?" Max asked hopefully.

"May we have dessert, please," his dad corrected.

"May we have dessert, please?" Max asked, an angelic smile on his face.

"Sure, you guys did great with dinner," their dad responded. "Ice cream? The one carton is almost empty and we need to finish it."

"I was thinking candy," Max responded casually.

Their dad exchanged looks with their mom. She nodded and he quickly put away his fingers he had flashed to her. "Go ahead and pick out two pieces," he said with an overly generous voice. The kids ran to their candy bins and each took out two pieces of chocolate candy. Claire dutifully gobbled down both pieces while Max enjoyed one and kept the other one at the table while he tried his best to savor the first piece. "Oh, whoops" said Claire as she wiped chocolate off her mouth, eyeing Max with guilty eyes.

"Oops, what?" her mother asked.

"Oh um… nothing," Claire shrugged.

As their parents began to clean up from dinner, Max took his second piece of candy and carried it upstairs to his room, safely tucking it under his bed along with some stuffed animals that had been there for weeks. He went to bed dreaming of chocolate covered ants.

The next morning after breakfast Max asked, "Can we go play Mud Café?"

"Have fun," his mom said with a smile.

Max walked cautiously, hoping his parents wouldn't notice the crinkling noise of the candy bar inside his pocket. Once outside, he raced to the withering ants. He opened the slightly melted candy bar and put it at the base of the tree stump. He squatted there for several minutes, watching to see if his chocolate buffet would take hold. It didn't take long at all for the ants to make their way over and begin forming a circle around the whole candy bar, nibbling with enhanced vigor. Claire strode over and squatted next to him without saying a word, as they both watched with delight as their army of ants feasted in the bright morning sun.

Days went by in an otherwise listless summer. Some neighborhood kids ran back and forth to each other's houses. Many families could be seen with straw hats carrying pool supplies down the street to go for a swim. But Max and Claire had one driving motivation each day, which was to watch the ants, to find scraps they might find useful, and to see to it that they didn't have to travel far for their daily dietary needs. The plastic cylinder by now was reinforced multiple times by more layers of plastic. There were thin sheets of tin foil warped into a sharp tip on the top. In fact, if their parents ever saw the tree stump and the ants' creation, they would probably pass it off for some fun project the kids themselves had made. They probably wouldn't stop to examine how intricate the inside craftsmanship was. It had a section where the ants had neatly organized a storage area of caramel and peanut pieces. There was a plastic bottle cap filled with water they had sealed shut with a piece of saran wrap that the kids had provided. And there were foil rows of chairs or beds that lined the insides that could fit hundreds, if not thousands of ants.

At the base of it all, there was a vast chamber that was some storage vessel and blocked from view. Inside must have been many small metal and wire pieces that the kids had provided but were nowhere to be seen. The kids thought they must have put them to use somewhere in the base of the structure.

"I think there's only one thing left we can give them," Max said squarely one Sunday morning.

"What?" Claire asked earnestly.

"Fuel for their rocket," he said, turning to her.

"Gas?" Claire said with disbelief.

"Why not? Daddy has some in the garage he uses for the lawn mower," Max reasoned. They looked up to the house. There was no sign of adults stirring.

Max walked to the garage, looked around, and took the small canister of gasoline out to the backyard, shoulders raised to his ears in fear of getting caught. He placed the canister carefully behind the stump, hoping the wood was wide enough to hide the canister from view. He ducked back behind the stump and wrestled with the cap until he was able to move it enough to get a strong blast of the smell of gasoline attacking his nostrils. He stood back, trying not to think of the trouble he would get in if he was caught.

"Kids!" they heard their dad yell from the back door. They both shot straight up and spun around, a panicked look of bewilderment on their faces. "Come get dressed! Hurry up, we're late for church!" their dad called impatiently.

Max thought furiously. By the time they left and got back from church, it would be almost two hours later. He didn't want to miss whatever was about to happen with the ants. Some of the ants had already walked over to the canister and were making their way up its side.

He ran inside, sweat beading on his forehead. "Daddy, I have to tell you something."

"Can you tell me while you wash your hands and get dressed?" his dad asked.

"Is there any way I can stay and watch these ants? They're doing something. They're building something. It's really weird," Max pleaded.

"Max, I love that you're interested but they'll still be building when you get back. They'll be building all summer."

"But Daddy," Max said, his voice rising. He paused. "It's a rocket. They're building a rocket. And I think they're done. I think they might blast off soon."

Max's dad stood up from picking up the morning pajamas off the floor and looked at his son. "I'm really excited to see this spaceship, but it will have to be after church. We are not missing church for whatever they're building. Don't forget to put on your socks." He strode off, gathering his keys, phone, and wallet. Max let out what felt like his last breath of air. Defeated, he took one last glance out the back window longingly.

"Sorry, Max," Claire said as she slipped her socks on and walked to the back door.

As the car pulled into the driveway after church, Max unbuckled his seatbelt and threw open the car door so hard it knocked into a bicycle. Claire scrambled out after him, pushing on the car door so hard the bicycle fell over. "Hey!" his mother cried, but Max was already sprinting towards the backyard, with Claire fast on his heels. They skidded to a stop at the stump, breathing heavily, their mouths twisted with confusion. There, on the stump, was a charred bundle of sticks and nothing else.

In the deafening silence, they heard the patient footsteps of their parents as they came up behind them and asked, "What did we miss?" There was no reply. Max and Claire had their necks craned up to the sky, their eyes filled with wonder.

The Moss Prophet

THE MOSS PROPHET

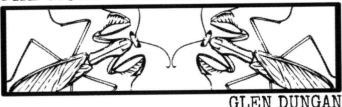

GLEN DUNGAN

The Moss Prophet's congregation hums in the ruins of a forgotten church, where vines creep upon ivory facades and wrap around broken glass panes. Long blades of thick grass are sticky with dewdrops that sway in the humidity of the open edifice. Warm water, the combined runoff from a neighboring swamp to the right and a crystalline stream to the left, engulf the cobblestoned floors with an inch of thick ichor where tiny bugs swim and vibrant bottle flies scuttle. There are no pews in the Moss Prophet's church. Instead, there are stumps and fallen logs that have been hallowed out by years of mass. In the corner of the open church, where the West side was blown apart during the forgotten war with the machines, a surviving wind chime twinkles in the swampy air. A frog croaks from the other side, booming through the kaleidoscopic orchestra of gnats and flies that swirl along the seats, singing in a language that only they can understand.

The midafternoon sun flutters from the marsh outside, warming the Moss Prophet as he waits submerged to his naval in the swamp water. His thick coat of moss and bark floats like limp wings along the murky water, and he feels the hardness of the cobblestones with his long, green toes. The texture is strange to the Moss Prophet, even now, even after all these years. Nothing in this forest is as hard as stone. Even the cement pillars have been reclaimed by the marsh, increasingly constricted by stringing vines, horned roses, and furry moss. An entire ecosystem, complete with its own politics and royalty exists on the pillar of the forgotten church. The Moss Prophet watches a water bug skate by, fanning tiny waves in between two lofty and approaching lily pads.

The wind chime sings underneath the wind that shook the bushes and grass. This sound was the Moss Prophet's favorite sound. He watched its rusty fingers clang together and waited for the congregation to start.

The first one to arrive was the Mantis Queen, accompanied by her sons. The Mantis Queen stood at eight feet. Her gown kissed the larger stumps as she passed. Her shell was not as immaculate as when she was young; shades of brown splotched along cracks where her biological body armor was beginning to brittle. The Mantis Queen was proud, and she held her head and her bladed arms high. She wore her weakness and age with dignity and continued to move with as much grace as a ballet dancer pirouetting and playing with ribbons. Her sons are broad chested, their shells greener than any of the moss in the congregation, and more vibrant than even the Moss Prophet's own skin, which was the color of steamed asparagus. They held their powerful arms to their sides and stood by the Mantis Queen's side as she settled herself into one of the stumps. Her sons are of age to take a wife and give the Mantis Queen a suitable heir. Each looks forward to watching the Mantis Queen's succession but has begun prematurely mourning for the cannibalization of their brothers.

The dull yellow light shining through the arch of the Moss Prophet's congregation preceded the second guest. The Lord of Lighting, brave leader of the Lightning Bug colony at the

North tip of the Marsh, floated along the water. The light from his body and crown illuminated the swampy waters below, showing the tadpoles and fish that traversed at the base of the stumps. The Lord took his seat next to the Mantis Queen, where his glowing body illuminated her left side. The Lord of Lightning did not come into the Moss Prophet's congregation alone; at the edge of the church grounds where the perimeter of the swamp encroached into a dark abyss there were faint orbs of yellow and orange underneath the awnings of trees. The Lord's knights preferred to stay back, making their own formidable perimeter of illumination. In the Moss Prophet's ruby peripheries, the lights dimmed and tossed light into the sky, thumping like heartbeats.

The final guest to arrive in the Moss Prophet's congregation was the proud and sturdy King Beetle. His purple armor shined as he waded his way through the murky water. A shawl of moss clung to his hardened shoulders. His horn spiked two feet above his fortified skull, and as typical birthright of the Beetle Kingdom delineation of royalty, his head had grown naturally to resemble a crown. Already his sons and daughters were checking the development of their scalps for any sign that a crown would emerge from their exoskeletons and the kingdom could ascend into a new generation. Yet, King Beetle remains old for he still has not found an heir and thus keeps making more children. There are rumors that perhaps the true heir to the Beetle Kingdom lay in the swamp, born to a poor mother in the muggy, humid air. The Moss Prophet hears many things and has seen a mother bring her daughter to the church that has the eyes of King Beetle. The King came alone, as he always does. He sat adjacent to the Mantis Queen and made sure not to brush against her delicate wings.

With all the guests in place, the Moss Prophet could properly begin his congregation. Against the dancing wind chime, the Moss Prophet blinked his red eyes and traced his long, slender fingers along the water. A cloud of gnats passed over them. He stood, revealing feeble and slender legs no thicker than the branches of a tree in winter. His long nose, almost a snout, dripped down his moss cloak and towards his stomach, curving into a hook. He licked lips the color of peas with a tongue the color of blood. Underneath his cloak, roses and tulips of yellow, white, and red breathed along his torso and ribs, blooming in and out like a palm opening and closing. They moved with his breath, and even in advanced age the Moss Prophet was proud of the unwiltering and unwavering quality of the flowers.

The Moss Prophet spread his arms wide and welcomed the Mantis Queen, the Lord of Lightning, and King Beetle to his broken church. The tribes in the insect kingdom were in constant conflict, as is the nature of territorial creatures. The Moss Prophet's role was not to sedate them, or to make them work together. Just four seasons ago the Mantis Queen and the King Beetle had threatened war with one another, and both had tried to convince the Lord of Lightning to lend a glistening hand. Two weeks prior one of King Beetle's daughters had abandoned the forest with one of the Lord of Lightning's most promising soldiers. No, the Moss Prophet's church was a sanctuary, just as it was for the SOFT ONE's before, just as it is for the insects who now rule the land. The Moss Prophet does not call his congregations summits. He calls them nothing. He does not send word to them, all guarded in their respective territories. They just arrive, unspoken, independent of the Moss Prophet. And he waits, because he knows they will come.

The Moss Prophet warned of a fourth guest, and the Mantis Queen dismissed the possibility with a wave of her bladed arm.

"How," she said, "can there be a fourth personality in the insect kingdom, when already we live in tumultuous, yet terrific balance?"

King Beetle scoffed and the Lord of Lightning fluttered his wings. King Beetle asked where a fourth kingdom could even fit in their forest land, and the Lord gestured that perhaps it was in the upper reaches where the trees are brittle and made of stone, where the SOFT ONES once had their caves and all the wind chimes lived.

The Moss Prophet shook his head and gestured to the entrance. The Mantis Queen's sons pivoted as the Lord of Lighting's guards illuminated a bright yellow, casting the entrance of the church in a dim marigold.

The unexpected guest walked in with an unsteady gait, favoring its right side. When it moved the sounds of metal scraping against rust filled the church. It wore a cloak of moss not unlike the Moss Prophet's or King Beetle's, but this cloak was strung together with vines and petals and was attached to the guest's overwhelmingly scarlet exterior just as how moss grows upon pillars. Its face had not pincers nor sharp teeth but a perfect circle with a tiny and reflective cracked surface. It had no claws or bladed arms and instead had three pronged fingers that looked like gnarled roots but were geometrically perfect. The guest waded through the water like a log floating downstream. It walked past the log pews and sat at the other end of the congregation, deliberate and alone. It moved with such lackluster intention that it made the Queen, the Lord, and the King collectively uncomfortable.

"This is no bug," the Mantis Queen clicked her pincers as her sons braced themselves with the curiosity. "Moss Prophet, explain yourself."

The Lord of Lightning scoffed and dismissed the creature with a wave of his hand. His body flashed yellow in disgust. "What creature is this, anyhow," the Lord said, "where are its claws, its many eyes? Why is its shell so flat and cold?"

King Beetle looked at the guest with reservation. He looked for a crown upon its head and found none. He said, "It is not royalty. It looks weak. Why did you bring the shiny monster here, Moss Prophet? Are the SOFT ONES rising from their mud to claim the Earth again?"

The Moss Prophet shook his head. He sat back down, feeling the tickle of the warm meniscus rise to his stomach, feeling the weight of his cloak lift and suspend on the surface. He gestured to the metal creature.

"This is a robot," he said, "a remnant of the SOFT ONES and the wars they used to kill each other. He was sleeping for over six hundred years, so much so that the forest has taken him in. Look! See the forest has grown upon his hard shell, claiming him."

King Beetle braced himself, puffed out his chest. The sons of the Mantis Queen followed.

"You've cursed us," the King said. "You've brought a weapon of war into our holy church, Prophet!"

"Silence," the Lord of Lightning said. "Curb your enthusiasm for battle, King Beetle. Not everything is a slight."

The Mantis Queen folded in her arms and rubbed the blades together. It sounded very much like the sound the robot makes when it moves. She said, "Let us see what it desires. What do you desire, robot?"

The robot turned, and the entire ecosystem living on its torso, arms, and legs, moved with it. DOES NOT COMPUTE, the robot said in a voice not full of little clicks or lapping tongues. WHERE ARE THE OTHERS IN MY UNIT? HAS THE OBJECTIVE BEEN COMPLETED?

The Mantis Queen shook her head. "It still thinks it's at war."

"Tell us of the SOFT ONES," the Lord asked.

SOFT ONES?

"Tell us of humans, the Moss Prophet said, "tell us of humans before they disappeared."

THERE ARE NO HUMANS IN THESE COORDINATES. HIGH LEVELS OF RADIATION DEEMED UNFIT FOR HUMAN SURVIVAL. GLOBAL TEMPERATURE HAS INCREASED CATASTROPHICALLY SINCE DEPLOYMENT. FOLIAGE INEDIBLE.

King Beetle asked, "Are there more of your kind? Perhaps hidden under logs or mud?"

ACTION UNAVAILABLE. CANNOT CONNECT TO CENTRAL COMMAND.

"It was a scout," the Lord of Lightning said. "I have them in my army, too."

"We know," the Mantis Queen said. "They are not very good."

The Moss Prophet turned to the rulers of forest. He spoke underneath the singing wind chime. "Do not fear the robot scout. It has awoken out of time. It is lost."

The Lord of Lightning's body illuminated in thought. Outside the perimeter of the church and past the open façade of its wall his guards communicated with one another using their electrified bodies. The Lord asked the Moss Prophet what should become of this robot, and if it does not get destroyed, should he be gifted with it as a memento of the SOFT ONES.

King Beetle scoffed, "The robot is a scout, not a gift. It should be in my kingdom. Its colors more closely match my shell anyway. It's destiny."

"Not quite" chirped the Mantis Queen, "you'll see its shell is red while you are purple. I vote that it remains with me, where it will be given a new purpose as one of my knights."

King Beetle growled and when he did, the Mantis Queen's sons put a hand on the hilts of their swords. He ignored them and asked if she planned for the robot to be eaten by the daughters of her kingdom, too.

The Mantis Queen stood, trailing her elegant cloak off the pool of water. The Lord of Lightning stood and flew up to the Queen's massive eight feet height. King Beetle joined them, and when he did both the Queen's sons and the Lord's guard surrounded them with their chests puffed. The Moss Prophet's church became invaded with aggressive clicks and clatters. It became enveloped in a ghastly yellow gloss. The Moss Prophet watched and waited. It was not his place to settle disputes. Although his congregation was a palace of upheld peace amongst the rulers of the forest, if they were to break this unspoken pact the Moss Prophet's existence would adapt to the new way of things, just as it had before and will after.

The robot turned. A spider crawled along its arm and disappeared underneath the large, capped fungi developing on its shoulder. THIS UNIT CANNOT REGISTER THE LIFEFORMS OF THIS ECOSYSTEM. Then it paused, and the three rulers and the Moss Prophet waited underneath another tickle of wind chime. After a second, the robot continued. THIS UNIT CANNOT CONNECT TO CENTRAL COMMAND. THIS UNIT CANNOT

PERFORM AUTONOMOUSLY. THIS UNIT SHALL PERFORM COMMAND: REST.

"Rest?" the Mantis Queen said. "No rest, metal creature. Not when your fate is being pulled in three ways."

King Beetle waded through the water and poked the robot in its circular eye. It did not recoil, and the lack of response made the King feel uneasy. He tapped it on its chest with a gauntleted finger.

THIS UNIT HAS ENTERED COMMAND: HIBERNATION & ERUPTION. THIS UNIT SHALL PERFORM COMMAND: ERUPT UPON CONDITION OF DEPARTING CURRENT LOCATION.

"You've angered it!" said the Lord of Lightning said. "King Beetle, the robot said it'll explode. Look what you have done!"

The King shook his head. "No. It has entered a sleep."

"And what if we move it?" said the Mantis Queen. "Will it explode if it leaves the Moss Prophet's church?

"It appears so," said the Moss Prophet, "this robot is a creature lost to time, purposeless, and afraid."

The Lord of Lightning asked if a creature such this even feels fear.

The Moss Prophet blinked. A tadpole bounced off his shrunken rib cage. "Yes. All creatures feel fear when they lose their purpose."

He looked to the robot, which now sat looking forward, ignorant of the three rulers of the forest who intended to claim it as an object. The Moss Prophet was unsure of his commanding voice, of how definitive he sounded when he made such efforts over these years to be a pacifist among the bickering rulers.

He continued, "The robot shall remain with me, for it is as old as the church, the last relic of the SOFT ONES that we have broken so far from. Let the robot be a reminder of how far we have come."

There was a silence amongst the three of the rulers, each who had not suspected the sudden decision-making from the Moss Prophet. Finally, the Lord of Lightning asked if the robot was a friend of all the forest.

"Yes," the Moss Prophet said. He leaned back and skated his fingers tips across the water. "I am tired now, my children of the forest. This congregation is over."

All three rulers, the Mantis Queen, the Lord of Lightning, and King Beetle, stood and made their way out of the entrance. They each gave the robot one fleeting glance before setting off into their respective colonies. The yellow glaze upon the church faded with the Lord.

The Moss Prophet stared at the robot, who had since taken another long sleep. It shall remain on this natural pew for eternity, for it will destroy the forest if it leaves. In a way, the Moss Prophet looked at the robot as a god of sorts, a deity forever tied to the forest and the church. The Moss Prophet will always have an audience of one, even after the Mantis Queen dies and her sons are cannibalized, long after King Beetle's bastard daughter rises to her throne, long after the Lord of Lightning's kingdom fades like the stars touching sunrise. And eventually, the Moss Prophet will die, leaving the flowers on his chest and stomach to wilt and crumble into the muggy waters.

Now, decades past, the robot remains sleeping, its moss cloak completely enveloping it, the mushrooms gripping its exterior now brown with rust. The robot, so foreign to the ways of life from the creatures who created its world and destroyed it, now becomes a part of the forest.

WORMQUAKE!

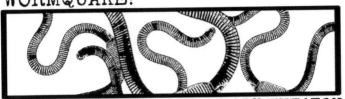

ELIZA WHEATON & MARK WHEATON

Remember, the blade for your Battle Bot needs 360-degree free movement, so make sure your servos—"

The robotics team coach, Ms. Hewlitt, was suddenly drowned out by a thunderous roar. The classroom shook. Windows rattled. Books tumbled from shelves. Water sloshed in the classroom aquarium. One of the dry erase boards popped off its hooks and slammed onto the ground.

Marlo Clark yawned and kept working on her robot.

A seventh grader at Goodall Middle School, Marlo had grown up in Southern California. Earthquakes, big and small, didn't bother her much.

"What do you think?" one of her classmates, Cass, asked when the rumbling stopped. "4.6? Epicenter in Tarzana?"

"Closer," a boy named Landon said. "5.0. Epicenter in Pacoima."

Marlo was about to counter when the school shook with such force it was like it had been struck by a wrecking ball. Two kids fell out of their chairs. Ms. Hewlitt grabbed the edge of her desk to keep from falling. This time, the shaking didn't stop.

Marlo shot a confused look around the classroom as the school seemed to bounce up and down on its foundation.

For an aftershock, it felt awfully like the building was being shaken from above rather than below.

"Whoa!" Landon called, staring out the window. "You have to see this!"

The day had started like any other.

Marlo's dad, a carpenter, was up before dawn and out the door just as Marlo was waking up. Her little brother, Ozzie, woke next and was playing video games when Marlo's mom rose a bit later.

"Can you walk Ozzie to school this morning?" her mom asked, drinking a third cup of coffee. "I have an early meeting."

"But Mom, he takes forever," Marlo protested.

"It's five extra minutes. Can I count on you?"

"Sure, Mom," Marlo said with a sigh.

Ozzie's school day started at 8. Marlo's at 8:10. Their schools, Attenborough Elementary and Goodall, were two blocks apart. A typical student could make it from one to the other with time to spare.

But Ozzie...

...took...

...forever...

...to get ready in the morning.

"Did you get dressed?" Marlo asked him at 7:43.

"Almost," he replied, playing a videogame in his underwear.

"Did you brush your teeth?" she asked at 7:45.

"Almost," he said, eating cereal, still in his underwear.

"Are you shoes on?" she asked at 7:52.

"Looking for socks," he replied, returning with a second bowl of cereal.

"Ozzie!" she yelled.

Somehow, she got him out the door by 7:59. Their house was only three blocks from school. If they ran, Marlo knew they could make it. But Ozzie kept stopping to rescue earthworms he found wriggling on the sidewalk.

"Come on, Ozzie!" Marlo chided.

"I can't leave them," Ozzie yelled, lifting two worms with a pair of pine needles. "They'll dry up in the sun!"

"We'll be late!" Marlo replied.

"It's not their fault," Ozzie said. "It's the stupid sprinklers!"

He wasn't wrong. Over the past two years, their neighborhood had been transformed. Old houses were demolished and replaced with gigantic, two-story monstrosities with little room left for yards. The oversaturating sprinkler systems stayed the same and routinely flooded earthworms out of their tunnels, the excess water pouring onto the sidewalks and into the street.

This, despite an ongoing drought so dire the city was now installing giant underground rainwater reclamation tanks in local parks, including the one at the back of their neighborhood.

People just did whatever they wanted to do.

"Pine needles aren't strong enough," Marlo said, taking out her house key. "Do it like this."

She gently slid her key under the first earthworm's middle, lifted it, and plopped it back onto the nearby grass. The second one didn't go easy, flailing and looping in on itself trying to get away. Marlo finally managed to get it onto the lawn as well.

"See?" Ozzie said. "We're not late."

Marlo rolled her eyes. It was 8:02.

"Get away from the window, Landon!" Ms. Hewlitt demanded.

"I'm serious!" he protested, pointing as the room kept shaking. "Look!"

Everyone flooded to the windows. Including Marlo.

Across the street in Marlo's neighborhood, every house under construction had either collapsed or was currently toppling even as the other houses remained upright. Great plumes of dust rose as the wood framing snapped like twigs.

That's not what caught Landon's attention.

"There!" Landon shouted.

Something massive wriggled between the houses. Marlo thought it was an eighteen-wheeler. Maybe two eighteen-wheelers? When it finally came into view, she gasped.

It was a giant earthworm. One the size of a freight train and easily a hundred yards long.

Marlo blinked in disbelief. When she opened her eyes, the worm was gone. She was relieved, worried she'd been hit on the head.

"Another one!" Cass cried.

A second worm rolled through a nearby fence as a third burst from a half-built swimming pool. Marlo was about to try her blinking trick again when a fourth squirmed down the street directly toward Attenborough Elementary.

Ozzie was in there, she realized.

She bolted for the door.

Panic ruled the streets. People ran in all directions, leaving their cars parked in the middle of the road to flee the rampaging earthworms. They crashed through stone walls, knocked over trucks, and flattened fences. Their movements shook the ground, almost knocking Marlo off her feet as she ran. She picked herself up and kept running.

She had to get to Ozzie.

One of the worms crawled out in front of her, blocking her way. She doubled back. Two more worms appeared behind her, boxing her in next to an apartment complex. The worms would be upon her in seconds, smooshing her into the building if she didn't get away.

She ran up the steps to the nearest unit and beat on the door. "Help! Let me in!"

No one answered.

She ran next door and tried again. Still nothing.

The worms were only yards away now. Marlo couldn't believe this was happening. There was a parking garage below the apartment building visible through grates alongside each apartment's stairs. She tried to open them. They held firm.

A horrifying wail erupted from the garage. Marlo clapped her hands over her ears as two dozen car alarms went off at once, their headlights blinking on and off at the earthworms' approach.

The earthworms reacted immediately. They slowed then backed away, driven off by the clamor. Marlo was relieved but surprised. Earthworms had ears?

Once the worms had gone, she looked back toward her brother's school. Several students were fleeing in the opposite direction from the worms. Only one child ran toward the worm-riven neighborhood.

It was Ozzie.

"Ozzie? Where are you?"

Marlo had seen her brother duck down their own street so she thought he'd gone home. But as she searched their house, he was nowhere to be seen.

The place was a mess, though from the initial earthquake or the rampaging earthworms she couldn't tell. Every plate and glass had tumbled from the kitchen cabinets. Bookshelves had fallen over. Her mother's plants had toppled in the hall.

"Ozzie?" she yelled, glancing out a back window.

The door to their detached garage was open. Ozzie was inside tearing apart loaves of bread and dropping the crumbs in their father's fertilizer spreader.

"Ozzie!" she cried, hurrying out the back door. "What're you doing? It's not safe!"

"We have to help the worms!" he yelled.

"What're you talking about? They're destroying the whole neighborhood."

"Not on purpose," Ozzie shot back. "That earthquake probably pushed them up out of the ground. We have to help get them back under before they dry up in the sun."

Marlo stared at Ozzie like he was nuts.

"How do you plan to do that?" she asked

"With this!" Ozzie said, raising the bread.

He crumbled up a piece and dropped it in the spreader. When he pushed the spreader, crumbs fired out in every direction.

"They'll follow the bread, right?" he said. "We can lead back where they came from!"

Marlo didn't think earthworms ate bread, much less would follow such tiny crumbs. Worse, the worms had come out of the ground at the various construction sites. All had collapsed after they'd emerged. They wouldn't be able to get back underground from there.

But maybe Ozzie was onto something. If they could find a way to herd the wor—

BOOM!

The back fence exploded into a million splinters. A giant worm crawled toward them through the wreckage.

"Back inside!" Marlo yelled.

Leaving the spreader and bread behind, Ozzie and Marlo ran into their house. A second worm slid across their front yard, blocking their escape.

Marlo had a plan.

"Make lots of noise!" she demanded. "Bang pots and pans. Blast music!"

"Siri, play loud music!" Ozzie cried.

Their kitchen speaker came to life blasting an opera at full volume. Marlo grabbed cookie sheets and slammed them together as Ozzie screamed and beat mixing bowls with a metal spoon. The noise was tremendous.

But the huge worm in the backyard kept inching toward the house.

"Louder!" Marlo commanded.

Ozzie beat the bowls with greater enthusiasm. Marlo screamed, too. The worm didn't seem to notice as it slammed into the wall of their detached garage, crumbling it. The house was next.

"Siri, do worms have ears?" Marlo asked.

"They don't," the kitchen speaker replied coolly.

So, what had frightened the worms by the apartment? Marlo wondered.

Then it came to her.

"Flash the lights on and off!" Marlo yelled.

"What?" Ozzie asked.

"They don't want to be in sunlight, right?" Marlo asked. "Light repels them!"

Ozzie dropped the bowls and ran through the house, blinking lights. Marlo did the same with the kitchen and porch lights.

To her surprise, it worked. The worm slowly altered course to avoid the lights, bashing through another fence on its way to the street. Marlo exhaled. They'd saved the house. Now, they had to save their neighborhood.

Marlo had an idea. It wasn't fully baked but worth a try.

"Ozzie? Where's your drone?"

Two summers ago, Ozzie had asked Marlo how streetlights knew to go on earlier at the end of daylight savings time. She'd looked it up on her phone.

"They have photo-resistors on top that signal the streetlight when it gets dark," she'd said, then forgot all about it.

Now that she needed to herd giant, light-averse earthworm, it came back to her.

"Your drone can pick up something small, right?" she asked Ozzie.

"Teeny-tiny," Ozzie admitted.

Marlo rooted through a laundry room drawer for markers. Each had dried out. She ran to her mother's room and grabbed a bottle of nail polish.

"Can it pick this up?" she asked.

"Um, sure," Ozzie replied, dubious.

They hurried to the garage only to find Marlo's bicycle crushed under the fallen garage wall. Ozzie managed to drag his own bike out and soon they were on their way, Ozzie perched on the handlebars, Marlo crouched on the too-small seat.

"Look, fire trucks!" Ozzie yelled as they zipped onto their street.

Sure enough, a long line of fire engines now stood between the worm-clogged neighborhood and the schools on the other side. The firemen unfurled their hoses as if hoping to repel the worms with water.

"Hey!" Marlo yelled as she cycled toward them. "Turn on your roof lights!"

The firemen looked at her in confusion.

"Your lights!" she repeated. "Turn on your lights!"

At that moment, one of the giant earthworms burst from the neighborhood and headed straight for Ozzie's school. Children were still being evacuated. The firemen raised their hoses to blast the worms. Marlo steered her bike into the worm's path.

"Now, Ozzie!" she said.

Using the remote control, he sent his drone skyward. Though it took a couple of tries, he finally managed to hover it over the streetlight closest to the worm. The nail polish brush hanging from its gimbal, he lowered it directly onto the flat photo-resistor, covering its sensor with polish. A second later, the streetlight blinked to life.

"You did it!" Marlo cheered, thinking her brother might make a welcome addition to her robotics team one day.

But the worm kept coming.

"Do the next one!" she yelled.

Ozzie hovered the drone over a second streetlight. When the light came on this time, the worm visibly recoiled. Not by much. Merely enough to tell Marlo it was working.

"One more," Marlo said.

Ozzie flew the drone over the last streetlight on the block and painted the sensor. When the light blinked on, the worm flinched again but still crawled forward. The streetlights weren't enough.

Suddenly, red and white lights flashed around her. A fire team, seeing what Marlo was doing, had turned on their engine's strobe lights. This time, the worm retreated. The other firemen quickly turned on their light as well then drove slowly into the neighborhood to pursue the worms.

Marlo cycled out ahead of them.

"Where are we taking them, kid?" a firefighter yelled.

"To the park!" she cried.

Though the city's water reclamation project had begun with surveys and soil tests months ago, the dig to excavate a space large enough to fit the reclamation tank had barely begun. A roped-off pit about thirty feet around and who-knows-how-deep stood where a soccer field had been, flanked by construction equipment. Marlo hoped the worms would use the pit's entrance to slip back underground.

The fire engines were doing an excellent job of herding the giant worms toward the park. Marlo and Ozzie continued to whiz along in front of them, turning on streetlights and making sure no earthworms slipped past in backyards or construction sites.

"Your plan's working!" Ozzie said, pointing to the last pair of worms retreating down the block.

The worms joined another dozen now wriggling their way around the park. Their bulky, viscous bodies turned over picnic tables, crushed a batting cage, and flattened a play structure. One worm crawled through a swing set that now rode on top of it like a strange metal hat.

But Ozzie was wrong. Marlo's plan wasn't working.

The worms went near the pit. Slid past its entrance. Knocked over construction equipment. But none entered.

"Why won't they go in?" Ozzie cried.

"Maybe they don't like the smell," Marlo said. "The construction equipment could be throwing them off."

Marlo stared at the giant creatures. With the sun rising high overhead, they were running out of time. Despite their destructive power, the worms were an incredible sight. It was like when her parents took her and Ozzie to see redwoods. They were like refugees from a prehistoric past long buried in the earth.

Which gave Marlo one last idea.

"Turn on your hoses!" she yelled to the firemen. "We have to soak the entire park!"

She cycled to the parks' sprinkler controls, the long, metal crank still in place from that morning. She imagined a worker abandoning it when giant worms sprouted from the ground. While the firemen turned on their hoses, Marlo turned on the sprinklers.

The ground soon looked as if a hurricane had come through. Six and a half acres of dirt quickly swirled into a maelstrom of mud. At first, the giant earthworms merely went from squirming along to sliding. Then, the ground beneath them emulsified into muck with the consistency of quicksand.

The worms began to sink.

A few tried to wriggle away. The firemen poured on more water. The pit collapsed in on itself, taking five worms with it. Others simply disappeared under the waves of muck, digging their way in deeper as they went.

"More water over here!" Marlo yelled, pointing to a dry patch near two worms.

The firemen soaked the ground. Soon, even this pair were submerged. The firemen cheered. Marlo grinned with pride.

Then plummeted into the earth.

The ground beneath Marlo's feet had collapsed. She was trapped in mud up to her nose before even realizing what was happening.

"Ozzie!" she yelled, mud pouring into her mouth and ears as she sank.

She tried to claw her way out, but it sucked her back down. Two firemen rushed over and grabbed for her hands, narrowly missing her fingertips. She was fully submerged in the grime. She kicked her feet, hoping to find a root or pipe. Anything she could push herself back up on.

There was only darkness and mud.

She felt something touch the soles of her feet. It was one of the worms. It gently lifted her skyward until her face broke through the surface of the mud.

"There!" a fireman shouted.

Two large hands grabbed Marlo and pulled her free.

"Are you okay?" Ozzie asked, hurrying over.

"I'm fine," she said, staring back into the pit, wondering if the worm gliding by had known it had saved her life.

"Is this...is this where the giant worms were?"

Under a tree in the park, Marlo looked up from her book. It was a couple of months later. Ozzie was nearby using his drone to take pictures of squirrels. The man standing in front of her had a camera in one hand, a metal detector in the other.

"Worms?" she asked, squinting.

"You know, giant earthworms," the man said. "The ones from YouTube."

"Ugh, that," Marlo said with a groan. "We had an earthquake. That was all."

"I saw the videos!" the man protested. "They're online."

"Those were fake," Marlo said. "Funny. But fake."

Ozzie wandered over. The man turned to him.

"You must've seen the giant earthworms, right?"

"Just fake ones online," Ozzie said, shrugging.

"Gah!" the man yelled, stomping off. "I drove all the way from Pittsburgh!"

Marlo waited until he'd left the park to shoot a grin at her brother. Ozzie grinned back and went looking for more squirrels. Marlo placed her hand on the ground.

From deep underground came a tiny, distant vibration in response.

ATTACK OF THE KILLER CENTIPEDE

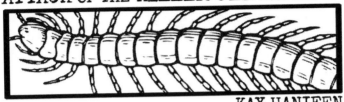

KAY HANIFEN

Some advice for my fellow Roosevelt Middle Schoolers: good friends don't wake you up in the middle of the night and best friends don't make you go with them to explore the abandoned lab off Graves Road. Just...don't go with them even if they call you a chicken and say you'll be out of the friend group and that they're gonna tell everyone that you like-like Bobby Graham when you don't because he picks his nose and snaps your bra straps. Trust me on this one. Even if you just moved to town and people think you're weird because you eat kimchi and noodles for lunch instead of peanut butter and jelly sandwiches. It's not worth it.

But here I was at the abandoned lab with a flashlight in the middle of the night while Meghan, her boyfriend, Mark, and Emily giggled and took pictures with the disgusting giant bug specimens still in their jars. I wrinkled my nose at the half-drunk cup of coffee still moldering in its mug. "People really left here in a hurry. What happened?"

Emily shrugged and drew a bad word in the dust on a computer monitor that looked almost as old as we are. "I was a baby when it happened. Mom and Dad used to work there. They said that there was a chemical leak or something that made it too dangerous for them to come back."

"But it's safe for us to explore," I said incredulously.

Something smacked the back of my head and I whipped around. Just a pencil. Meghan giggled in Mark's arms. "Don't be such a worry-wort. You'll make us all depressed."

I rolled my eyes. "Fine. But if we get killed by a chainsaw wielding maniac, that's on you."

"You watch too many scary movies," Meghan said.

"And you don't watch enough. Trust me, something bad'll happen and if we survive, we'll be grounded for the rest of our lives."

"Don't be so dramatic," Mark said, "Nothing bad's gonna happen."

As if on cue, we heard an "oops" from Emily who had wandered into the next room and the sound of scraping furniture. "Hey guys, check this out!" she called.

Against my better judgement, I followed the disgustingly lovey-dovey couple into the next room where there was a secret door. Something about this lab didn't sit right. I saw a lot of bug experiment samples, but nothing so dangerous that it would make them completely abandon the place. What chemical were they even working with?

If I'm being honest, I hate bugs. A lot. They have too many legs and I know they're necessary for the environment, but they're still gross. Except for ladybugs and butterflies. They're pretty, so I give them a pass. Most of the bug specimens we found were of giant centipedes, and those are the worst. I hate that they have so many legs and venomous forcipules and scuttle out of the shadows like they enjoy scaring us.

Even though they were dead and locked away in jars of formaldehyde, they made me incredibly uncomfortable. I used to read a lot about bugs as a form of exposure therapy. Fear and fascination made them a sort of obsession. Know thy enemy, right? Well, according to the books I read, centipedes can grow up to a foot long, which is horrifying enough on its own, but these were at least double or even triple that. Were they experimenting with making bigger bugs? Why would they do that?

When we reached Emily, she was shining her light down a staircase that had been hidden behind a bookshelf like a *Scooby Doo* episode. "What do you think's down there?" she asked.

Mark grinned. "Only one way to find out."

I shook my head. "Nope! No thank you! There's no way you're getting me to explore the secret mad science chambers. Nuh uh."

Meghan rolled her eyes. "Don't be lame, Kira."

"Don't be suicidal, Meghan. This is the part of the movie where we accidentally unleash a zombie plague or a kaiju or a demon or something."

"She has a point," Mark said, "It's one thing to explore this floor. Everyone does it. But we don't know what mad science they got up to down there."

"Well, I'm going," Emily said, skipping down the stairs. Meghan and Mark shrugged to each other and followed after her.

My mom always told me to listen to the little voice in my head when it tells me something's wrong. She says it's saved her life several times. But if I was good at listening to my mother, I wouldn't be trespassing in an abandoned lab in the middle of the night, so I followed them despite the alarm bells blaring in my head. The one alone always gets picked off first, especially if you're not white. I made sure to grab a pair of scissors from the desk, though, in case there was a murderer in the secret basement. I could hear them up ahead snickering and whispering and I stopped short. I was never close to them, so why were they so insistent that I come tonight? And how did Emily find this secret passage? They were planning something, probably going to lock me in and try to scare me as a prank. Well, I wasn't as easy of a mark as they thought. I don't care if they say I like Bobby Graham. Whatever they're plotting will probably be so much worse than middle school boys being perverts.

"Nope," I whispered and turned heel, heading out of the lab building and to my bike. Maybe I'll get lucky, and Mom and Dad won't notice I was gone. Ha. Fat chance.

There were shrieks coming from inside the building, but I ignored them. They were probably just trying to scare me into making sure they were okay so they could spring the trap. Well, I wasn't falling for it.

But then Meghan and Emily came barreling out the door, tears streaming down their faces. "It got Mark," Meghan wailed.

"It ate him like an appetizer," Emily added, equally hysterical.

I rolled my eyes. I'd seen better acting in my fourth-grade school play. "Yeah right. I know you're just trying to scare me."

Emily was clutching her hair, muttering something like, "I can hear it calling to me in the back of my head. I've heard it for so long it's like it chose me. Like I'm a prophet, but it doesn't want me to preach. It wants to eat and eat and eat and eat and eat…"

Ignoring her, I put on my bike helmet and mounted the bicycle. "Tell Mark it's not gonna work."

"Fine! We were going to like, lock you in a closet or something, but I swear I'm not making this up. It's gonna kill us all."

Emily stiffened, going completely still like someone pressed her pause button. "It's coming," she whispered.

And something massive burst from the lab, forcipules clicking and legs skittering. The centipede had to be forty feet long, with a reddish-brown body and black and yellow legs. I mounted my bike. "Run!"

Emily and Meghan hopped onto their bikes, and we pedaled as fast as our legs would allow. The giant centipede was closing in on us. Lungs and legs burning, I wracked my brain as to how to stop this thing. They had to hide in cool, moist places because they lacked a waxy cuticle that most insects and arachnids had. If they were separated from those two things, they'd dry out.

"To the gas station," I shouted.

"Why?" Meghan shouted back.

"I have a plan." If there's one thing that I dislike more than bugs, it's fire. I've always been a little scared of its destructive power, how it can cause so much pain so easily, but apparently tonight was a night for facing fears.

We turned onto a paved road. The 7-11 was maybe a five-minute ride away if we could make it that far. The sound of chitin scraping against asphalt set my teeth on edge. "Don't you hear it calling to us?" Emily shouted, "It wants us."

"I don't hear anything," Meghan said.

"Didn't she say her parents used to work at the lab?" I asked.

"Yeah." While she was keeping pace, Emily was falling behind. Meghan glanced over her shoulder. "She was the one who suggested that we go there."

That was weird. Her parents were obviously mad scientists. Had they somehow made Emily psychically connected to the centipede? I didn't dare say anything more. My lungs and legs burned, and I needed to focus on pedaling.

Finally, the lights of the 7-11 appeared like angels from heaven. We turned to go into the gas station and dismounted the bikes on jelly legs, locking the doors behind us. Meghan pulled Emily to a corner where she rocked back and forth while muttering about hearing it calling to her and that she had to bring us there to get the voice to stop. The cashier, who had been asleep at his post, blinked awake. "Hey, what are you...?" He spotted the giant centipede. "Holy fudge!" Except he didn't say fudge. I'm just too polite to repeat a swear word.

I grabbed a lighter and an aerosol can. "We need your help to start a fire," I said, cringing as the centipede crashed into the gasoline pumps. The overpowering odor filled the air, making me dizzy.

The cashier grinned. "Sweet! I've always wanted to burn this place to the ground." It crashed into the glass at the front, and we all cried out in terror. He leapt over the counter and said, "There's a back door. Come on!"

With Meghan dragging Emily, we sprinted out the back. The creature, trying to follow us, thrashed, breaking displays and sending gasoline everywhere. I struggled with opening the aerosol can while the cashier lit the lighter. "You kids get a safe distance away," he said, puffing out his chest and giving us a cocky grin like he was some kind of action hero instead of an acne covered college student. In its thrashing, the giant centipede's body slammed into him, sending him flying a good ten feet. The lighter went out as it hit the ground. Meghan went to go check on him while I stared at the lighter. It was too dangerous to go in for another one, and we didn't have anything else to use to start a fire. So I, in my infinite intelligence, scurried in between the legs and its body, grabbing the lighter and rushing back out of range again. It rammed into me, sending me flying like the cashier. But I was more ready than him. I landed on the hard asphalt, breaking my fall by tucking and rolling. It knocked the breath from my lungs and my skin stung all over. I was probably super scraped up, but I held onto the lighter and aerosol.

With shaking fingers, I flicked it on, staring at the orange glow for a moment before spraying the aerosol can, creating a makeshift flamethrower like I saw on a YouTube video. The flames caught and the creature shrieked, thrashing about in agony as it was quickly engulfed. I ran, terrified of getting hit by a giant flaming centipede. Vaguely, I could hear Emily screaming as well, and smelled something sort of like fried shrimp.

Soon, the thrashing stopped, and it laid dead. We sat on the grass watching the smoldering remains while the cops, ambulance, and fire department swarmed the scene like ants. They took Emily away in a straitjacket and the cashier on a stretcher. He was still alive but had a nasty concussion. Meghan and I sat waiting for our parents to pick us up.

"Do you really think Emily tricked us there just to feed it?" she asked.

I shrugged. "I'm not sure." Staring at the charred beast, I felt something I hadn't expected: pity. "I mean, they just left it alone and alive down there. If it could link to her telepathically, then it clearly was intelligent and starving. I kind of feel bad for it."

Meghan gave me an incredulous look. "Kira, you are so weird."

I sighed, resting my chin on my knees. "I know." Picking up my head, I grinned. "But weird just saved your life."

Meghan let out a huffy half-chuckle. "Okay fair."

We sat for a while watching the sunrise. Soon, our parents would show up and ground us for all eternity, but for the moment, I just took in the cool air, the morning dew, and the smell of gasoline cooked centipede and was grateful in that moment that at least I was alive.

The Bug Whisperer

THE BUG WHISPERER

KEVIN HOPSON

Harrison sat at his computer, combing through a never-ending list of emails when the doorbell rang. He glanced out the window, noticing a sedan parked along the street in front of his house.

Harrison stood from his chair and walked out of the bedroom, making his way toward the top of the stairs. They led down to the first-floor foyer, and he could see the back of his mother at the bottom of the steps.

She held open the door, but Harrison couldn't get a good view of the visitor. He sidestepped the railing and put a shoulder to the wall, staying out of sight while eavesdropping on their conversation.

"I'm Detective Isabel Barnes," the visitor said. "Are you Mrs. Skinner?"

"Yes," his mother replied. "Is there a problem?"

"There's no problem," Isabel said. "Nothing involving you, at least. But I'm sure you heard about Violet Coleman, the eight-year-old girl that went missing yesterday."

"Of course."

"I'm not sure how much you know about it, but she ventured into the woods, and her parents are desperate to find her."

"I know she went missing," Harrison's mother said, "but I didn't realize she wandered into the woods." There was a pause. "*The* woods?" she asked.

"Unfortunately," Isabel said. "Her parents were brave enough to go after her, but they were chased from the woods shortly after entering."

"I'm afraid to ask, but what chased them away?"

"A giant wasp," Isabel answered. "We had some officers that volunteered to search as well, but all of them met the same fate as Violet's parents. Some of them were even attacked and sustained injuries. The woods are a very dangerous place, as I'm sure you're aware."

"Yes."

"Which is why I'm here," Isabel said.

A brief period of silence followed.

"You're going to ask me about Harrison," his mother eventually said.

"I wouldn't normally do this type of thing, but time is of the essence, and he's the best chance we have at finding her."

His mother let out a breath. "I can understand your predicament and, as a mother, I can surely sympathize with Violet's parents. But if Harrison were to do this, the entire town would be lining up at my door. He's constantly harassed by people trying to take advantage of him. He's still a teenager, and I want him to enjoy these last years before college." She hesitated. "Plus, I'd be lying if I didn't say that I fear for his safety."

"I understand your concern, Mrs. Skinner. As I said, if there was any other way—"

"I'm sorry," his mother said. "I can't help you."

Harrison quickly made his way to the top of the stairs. "Mom."

She spun around and stared back at him.

"It's okay," Harrison said.

He descended the staircase, eventually sidling up to her.

"I overheard your conversation," Harrison said to Isabel. He glanced at his mother, then turned his attention to Isabel. "If you need my assistance, I'm willing to help."

"Harrison," his mother said with anxiety in her voice. "I can't let you do this."

"I'll be fine, Mom," he insisted. "I know it's hard for you, but imagine what Violet's parents are going through right now."

She shook her head, and tears slid down her face. "I've already lost one son. I can't afford to lose you, too."

Harrison looked down at his mother, meeting her gaze. "Sometimes you have to have faith in me."

"I do."

"Then let me help. I've obviously done this before. If I had any doubts, I wouldn't offer to do it."

The three of them stood in silence.

"Fine," his mother finally said. She looked to Isabel. "But you will protect my son at all costs."

Isabel nodded. "Of course, Mrs. Skinner. I promise."

Isabel drove him to a nearby park. It was about a half-mile from Harrison's house, and he spotted the edge of the forest as Isabel pulled into the small parking lot. The woodlands stretched for a few miles, and there were various entry points. But, according to Isabel, this is where Violet was last seen before wandering off.

It made sense to search this area of the forest first, especially since people rarely made it far once they ventured inside. The park resembled a ghost town now. Few people visited given the forest's new residents, and it had been that way for months. No one knew what caused the bugs to grow to such an incredible size.

A military base and a nuclear power plant were only miles away, so many put the blame on one or both of them. Radiation perhaps. But if that were the case, why weren't the larger animals impacted? And why weren't people getting sick? A more plausible explanation was a military experiment. But even that was a stretch.

Whatever the reason, Harrison found it amazing. His infatuation with bugs is what spurred him to brave the forest while most of the townspeople preferred to steer clear of it. In fact, more and more of the town's residents were moving away. The initial influx of scientists, government agencies, and military personnel didn't help either.

Even some of the country's greatest minds couldn't find a way to conduct research without being attacked and chased from the woods. Most of the outsiders eventually left, but some stuck around to further their investigation. When it was learned that Harrison could trek through the forest without issue, he was sought out by many of these same people.

Given the size of the bugs, there wasn't much Harrison could do in terms of obtaining physical evidence for scientists and other interested groups. On a few occasions, however, he wore a body camera and made note of what he encountered, passing along this information to the proper people before Harrison's mother finally put an end to it.

Isabel sighed as the two of them stood at the edge of the woods.

Harrison studied her. He'd never been good at guessing a person's age, but he figured Isabel was in her thirties. And she appeared to be a fit woman, which didn't come as a surprise given her profession.

"Have you ever done this?" he asked.

She turned to him, her brown ponytail twirling through the air. "Ventured into the woods?"

Harrison nodded.

"Not in months. Not since things took a turn for the worse," she elaborated.

"Have they?"

"Have they what?"

"Taken a turn for the worse?" he said.

"I suppose it isn't the case for someone like you, but it is for practically everyone else in this town."

Harrison could understand.

"How do you do it?" she asked. "Go through the forest unscathed?"

He could only shrug. "I don't have an answer. It's not as if I have telepathy or something and can talk to them. For whatever reason, they leave me be, and I do the same with them." Harrison scanned the trees. "Maybe bugs are similar to other animals. The ones that can sense fear. Maybe they feed off of it."

"Not literally, I hope."

Harrison managed a smile.

"I don't like bugs in the first place," Isabel said. "So, you can imagine my fear of running into one that's even bigger than me."

"Just stay close," Harrison said. "Hopefully, they'll give you a free pass if you're with me."

"That's why I brought you along, but what if the bugs have other plans?"

Harrison lowered his gaze to Isabel's belt. "You have a gun. I wouldn't suggest using it unless it's an emergency, but it can be our backup plan." He took a moment to collect himself. "Ready?"

Isabel gave a nod.

"Which direction?" he asked.

Isabel pointed. "How about that way?"

Harrison obliged, and the two of them walked together. He took a slight lead, staying ahead of Isabel by a step or two.

It was a cool and overcast day. Though the leaves had only recently started to change color, some had already lost their battle with Mother Nature. A few crackled beneath his weight as he guided Isabel deeper into the forest. Most of the trees in this part of the forest consisted of pines, but Harrison noticed some birch, hickory, and cedar trees along the way as well.

He kept an eye out for anything and everything. The bugs would be easy enough to spot, so he focused on the forest floor instead, inspecting the area around his feet as he walked. Harrison wasn't sure what he was looking for, but that was okay. Sometimes things had a way of finding him.

He glanced over his shoulder at Isabel. Her head turned as if it were on a swivel, constantly examining the forest. And she cowered as she moved, staying low to the ground, obviously troubled at what may be lurking nearby.

A buzzing came from overhead, and a breeze tugged at Harrison's hair as the noise grew louder. He looked up to see a flying insect. It glided past them, and Isabel let out a shriek. She dropped to the ground, resting on her belly.

"It's only a damselfly," Harrison said.

"A what?" she said, panting.

"Similar to a dragonfly but thinner."

"And you can tell the difference?"

He nodded. "Instead of thinking of them as oversized bugs, just pretend we're looking at them through a microscope."

Isabel exhaled. "I guess that's one way of approaching it."

Harrison offered her a hand, and Isabel gripped it. He pulled Isabel to her feet.

"You okay?" he asked.

"Yeah. Thanks."

Harrison turned away, spotting something in the distance. "Okay," he said calmly. "Don't freak out."

"Oh, God! What?"

He pointed. "Straight ahead. Check out the web between those two oak trees."

"Holy—" She stared with wide eyes. "That spider is as big as a bus."

"That's not a spider," Harrison commented. "At least, not the larger of the two figures that you see on the web."

"I don't understand."

"It's a decoy spider. They gather dead prey and debris from their surroundings and use it to build a giant replica of themselves. That's what you see in the middle of the web. Above it is the actual spider."

Isabel gasped. "It's still huge." She took a moment to ponder. "What's the reason for building that?"

"To scare away predators," Harrison replied. "Some predators won't eat spiders if they're too big. The damselfly, for example. It makes sense that we just saw one. It probably thought twice about its meal after seeing that decoy."

Harrison inspected the web from afar.

"What was Violet wearing when she disappeared?" he asked.

"Blue jeans and a pink blouse, I think. But let me check my notes." Isabel pulled a cell phone from her pants pocket and navigated the screen. "Yeah. Exactly as I said."

"What does that look like to you? In the decoy?"

He watched as Isabel squinted.

"I'm not sure what I'm supposed to be seeing," she said, "and I refuse to get any closer to that thing."

"The pink. You can see it from here."

Isabel stretched her neck to look. "Okay. I see it now." She raised an eyebrow. "Are you implying that it's a piece of Violet's blouse?"

"I'm not sure, but I don't think pink is a common color to find in a spider web. Since the spider collects things from its environment, it's possible it came from Violet's blouse, which means she could be nearby."

"What if the spider—" Isabel swallowed, not wanting to finish her question.

Harrison already knew what she was thinking, but he refused to go down that road. Not yet, at least.

"Let's not assume the worst," he said. "Let's scope the area. If it is a piece of her blouse, it could have caught on something and torn off while she moved through the woods."

Isabel nodded and proceeded to search the area, Harrison following suit. He inspected low-hanging branches and brush to see if any clothing had stuck to them. Harrison continued the hunt for several more minutes, but he failed to find anything.

"Any luck?" he asked Isabel.

She shook her head. "Nothing. I can't even find footprints."

It made sense. The ground was dry and hard, and part of the forest floor was covered in leaves.

"Hello," a voice called out.

Harrison's eyes bulged. "Hello," he replied, speaking loud enough for them to hear but not so booming that it stirred the spider or any other bugs in the vicinity.

"Where's it coming from?" Isabel asked.

"To my left."

Harrison waited patiently.

"Hello," the voice said again.

"Yeah," Harrison said. "It's definitely that way. West."

Isabel sidled up to Harrison, and the two of them headed in that direction.

"We're coming," Harrison said.

He walked with urgency, Isabel keeping pace with him. Harrison fought his way through some heavy brush and when he went to step over a Buckeye shrub, he nearly lost his footing. That's because a sink hole appeared only a few feet away. He extended his arm out to the side, making sure Isabel didn't fall victim to it.

"Hello," Harrison said.

"Down here," the voice said.

From a distance, Harrison couldn't tell if the voice was male or female, but now it was clear. It sounded like a girl's voice.

"Violet?" he said.

"Yes."

Harrison sidestepped the hole and bent over to look. He could see a silhouette in the darkness and some of Violet's facial features as she stared up at him.

"Do you have a flashlight?" he asked Isabel.

"Sure," she replied.

Isabel pulled one from her belt and aimed the light at the hole.

"Anyone coming from our direction would never see the hole until it was too late," Harrison murmured to Isabel. "The shrub hides it, and I nearly stumbled into it myself."

"I hurt my ankle," Violet said, "and it's too high to climb."

Harrison studied the hole. It was about ten feet deep. Not an impossible climb for someone his height but definitely a challenge for an eight-year-old girl.

"If I lower my hand, do you think you can grab my arm?" he asked.

"I think so," Violet said.

Harrison put his chest to the ground and hung over the side, extending his arm. Violet clutched his wrist. He wasn't strong enough to pull her out with one arm, and if he tried to use his free arm to help, Harrison would surely lose his leverage.

"I need your help," he said to Isabel.

"What do you need me to do?" she asked.

"Drop the flashlight and grab hold of my ankles. I need you to anchor me."

Isabel rested the flashlight along the edge of the hole. It was no longer shining on Violet, but it still provided some light. She circled around and grabbed both of Harrison's ankles.

"Okay," he said to Violet. "I'm going to grab your wrist with my other hand and try to pull you up."

Harrison successfully grasped her wrist, but he slid forward, immediately fearing the worst. Then he felt Isabel's hands tighten around his ankles. He mustered all of the strength he could, slowly pulling Violet closer.

"I'm going to pull you," Isabel said.

"Do it," Harrison replied. "She's almost to the top, but I can't pull her out without shifting my legs."

Harrison's body gradually slid backward along the ground, and he kept hold of Violet with both hands. Her head reached the top of the hole, and Violet used her free hand to grip the ground beside him.

"Almost there," Harrison said.

Isabel continued to pull, and Violet finally emerged, Harrison steering her clear of the hole. Violet crawled to his side, and Isabel crouched beside them, offering a smile.

"Good work," Harrison said, panting.

"Same to you," Isabel huffed.

He eyed Violet. She had a few smudges on her dark skin, but she looked healthy otherwise. Then he remembered her ankle.

"Do you think you can walk?" he asked.

Violet got to her feet. She stood with a lack of confidence and limped as she took a few short steps.

"I'll limp home if I have to," she said, obviously relieved.

"And I'll carry you home if I have to," Harrison said with a grin.

Violet smiled in return.

"Harrison?" Isabel interrupted.

"Yeah."

"Turn around."

He glanced over his shoulder, his brows arching at the sight. The spider was out of the web. And it was coming toward them.

Harrison stood. "Get behind me. Both of you."

They did as he said, and Harrison watched as the spider neared. He hoped it would turn back, but the spider continued to advance.

"I'm not sure what to do," he said. "Other than run."

He heard a snapping noise from behind. Harrison glimpsed Isabel. Her holster was open, and she held a gun at her side.

"No," he said. "There must be another way."

"If there is," Isabel replied, "I'd like to hear it. Do you really think we can outrun it?"

Harrison had to be honest with himself. Given the size and the speed of the spider, the odds of outrunning it were slim at best. Then he felt something brush his shoulder. It was Violet. And she took a step toward the spider.

"Violet," Harrison hissed. "What are you doing?"

He was about to grip Violet's shoulder and reign her in when the spider came to a stop. Violet did the same. Then she raised a hand and waved.

"Thank you," she said to the spider.

Much to Harrison's surprise, the spider turned and headed back to the web.

Violet spun around to face him. "She kept me company last night and was probably just checking on me. I don't think she meant us any harm."

Harrison's mouth hung agape, and he looked to Isabel. "I guess I'm not the only one with the gift."

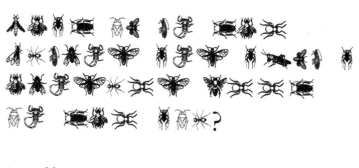

ANGST OF AN ATOMIC ANT

RUFA FORMICA

Dr. Mayhem loomed over me as he adjusted the dials on an enormous machine. A beam of pulsing radiation inched closer and closer to me. Of course, at that moment, I didn't know his name, or even what a name was. Nor did I know what I dial was, or a machine, or radiation. How could I? I was only a tiny ant, with an infinitesimal brain, so small that Dr. Mayhem had required an electron microscope to cut open my carapace and implant almost invisible specks of metal and silicon into my rudimentary nervous system.

Then, *ZZZAP!* The radiation beam focused on me. The chemicals surrounding me in the petri dish vaporized. My carapace burned as the quantum computing microchips grafted onto my nerve cells soaked up all the energy being fed to them.

For a few minutes, everything was confusion. For reasons I couldn't yet comprehend, I was suddenly imbued with the knowledge of what words like "infinitesimal" and "rudimentary" meant. Worse, my point of view shifted, leaving me dizzy and discombobulated as all the objects around me became smaller and smaller.

Dr. Mayhem, who'd towered over me like a titan mere seconds before, shrank until he was only twice my size, then exactly my size, then half my size. When the shrinking

93

stopped, *I* was towering over *him*, with my head pressed against the metal roof of the abandoned warehouse where he'd built his laboratory. It was then I understood that Dr. Mayhem and his equipment hadn't gotten smaller; I'd gotten bigger. Enormous! Colossal! Gargantuan!

Monstrous.

The realization of what I'd become flooded into me as I grappled with self-awareness for the first time. Dr. Mayhem had transformed me into a creature thirty feet tall and at least a hundred feet long. The quantum microchips grafted to my nervous system boosted my intelligence a million times over.

Despite the insights provided by my newborn intellect, I couldn't guess why Dr. Mayhem had not only turned me into a monster, but also made me a genius.

Though I had no vocal cords, I instinctively rubbed my middle leg against my abdomen, creating vibrations to produce sound. The torrent of new vocabulary gushing into my enhanced brain told me this process was called "striation." It took me only a few seconds to fine tune the vibrations until they formed the word, "Why?"

"Why?" Dr. Mayhem asked, his eyes narrowing as his lips curled into an evil grin. "For revenge, of course! Revenge against all those who mocked my genius! Revenge, most of all, against Mother Justice and the Virtue Battalion for daring to imprison me! All because I robbed a bank or two in order to fund my vital research! My embiggening ray could have changed the world! You, my greatest creation, shall make them pay for their insolence!"

I striated my abdomen once more. "I mean, why did you make me intelligent? Knowing what I've become is pure agony. Only a few hours ago, I was a worker in a colony, laboring alongside half a million brothers, faithfully serving our queen. Now, I'm alone, the first and last of my kind. You created me as an instrument for mindless destruction, then gave me a mind that comprehends my isolation? Was it mere cruelty that you inflicted me with this accursed knowledge?"

Dr. Mayhem shook his fist at me. "I certainly didn't give you intelligence so that you could ask foolish questions! By now, your quantum brain should have deduced the truth! Cease your prattling! It's time for you to trample my enemies into the dust!"

I tilted my head, gazing upon my creator through faceted eyes. There was something odd about my eyes, beyond the fact they were now several yards across. Each facet of my eye was seeing the world in different spectrums of energy. I could see the electrochemical impulses flowing in Dr. Mayhem's brain. My bio-electric intellect quickly deciphered these signals, decoding them by performing a quintillion equations in zeptoseconds. In enlarging my body, Dr. Mayhem had burdened me with so much mass I shouldn't have been able to stand under my own weight. He'd enhanced my brain to trigger latent psychokinetic powers. My power of mind-over-matter gave me unfathomable strength to crush Dr. Mayhem's foes. My self-awareness and alienated angst over what I'd become were merely unwanted side effects.

With my newfound intelligence being only a few minutes old, I had no emotional tools to handle the rage growing within me. I hated what I'd become, and hated the world that made my existence possible. Dr. Mayhem wished for me to destroy things? Well, why not? My mere existence was proof that there was no justice in the universe. Trampling a city into dust wouldn't solve my existential crisis, but it might provide welcome catharsis!

Before I could unleash my wrath upon my first and most obvious target, there was a bright flash, followed by thunderous *BOOM!* My fore-legs were the size of tree trunks but still not wide enough to shield my eyes from the glare as the white hot molten remains of the roof fell into the room. The flaming slag splattered on my chitinous thorax. I reared onto my hind-limbs in pain, which tore away even more of the warehouse roof.

In the sky above me were three humans, a tall woman with her eyes covered by a blindfold, a burly man with a jetpack and camouflage fatigues who carried what looked like a cannon, and a slender girl with neon blue hair who flitted about the sky, her blurred limbs emitting a loud buzz.

"It's over, Dr. Mayhem!" the blindfolded woman called out. "Hummingbird, grab the doctor! Thundergun, keep his monster busy!"

Before I could rub my abdomen to form the word "wait," the man with the huge gun took aim and pulled the trigger. There was another blinding flash and deafening clap of noise. Something slammed into my thorax, knocking me backward. I flailed about, completely blind and deaf. Ants don't have ears; we sense sounds by feeling vibrations in our legs. Right now my entire exoskeleton was ringing like a bell. I writhed on my back in helpless confusion.

Fortunately, my discombobulation lasted only a fraction of a second. The quantum circuits grafted to my nerves processed information at the speed of light. I swiftly remembered that the entire purpose of this circuitry was to empower me with telekinesis. With a thought, I silenced my ringing carapace and floated up into the air, righting myself. By willpower alone, I reset the photoreceptors in my light-blasted eyes to restore my vision.

Thundergun took aim at me once more, plainly consternated that his first shot hadn't finished me off. This time, before he could pull the trigger, it was a simple matter to pulverize every bone in his fingers with but a thought.

With a tiny bit more concentration his entire gun fell apart into a pile of fragmented metal.

"A little help here!" Thundergun screamed, holding his injured hand. He looked up at the blindfolded woman floating overhead; Mother Justice, I presumed. "This monster is tougher than it looks!"

"Tougher, smarter, and even more enraged than I was before you showed up," I shouted as I rose higher. I no longer even needed to rub my abdomen to make sound. I could simply vibrate the air with my mind to give voice to my agonized thoughts. "You attacked without provocation! You fear what you don't understand!"

"We understand you're a mutant abomination created by a madman to destroy everything in its path!" shouted Thundergun.

"Hmm," I said. "I suppose humans can also fear what they *do* understand. And rightly so! I'll destroy you all… once I've killed the monster that created me!"

With a speed that no doubt surprised my attackers, I flew toward Dr. Mayhem, my mandibles opening wide, intending to snap him in half. The blue-haired girl, Hummingbird, buzzed in from the side and grabbed the deranged scientist, zipping him clear of my snapping bite.

Fast as she was, Hummingbird could never fly faster than the speed of thought. With my faceted, multi-spectrum vision, I could see her muscles and skeleton moving in concert to create her rapid flight. With no effort at all, I willed the tendons of her left rotator cuff to rip.

Hummingbird cried in pain as she plummeted. Inches from the floor, Thundergun zoomed in with his jet pack and caught her and Dr. Mayhem. Annoyed, I ruptured the fuel line of Thundergun's jetpack. Flames flew back along his legs as the three of them corkscrewed into a high speed spin before smashing through the far wall of the warehouse. Thundergun twisted his body at the last second, either by chance or design, to take the brunt of the impact.

From the tangle of bodies that now lay beyond the wall, Dr. Mayhem rose on trembling legs. I floated toward him, watching his eyes go wide with terror.

Mother Justice drifted down from the heavens, placing herself between me and my accursed creator.

"That's enough," she said, holding her upraised palm toward me. "I can't let you kill Dr. Mayhem."

"Why not?" I demanded. "He's your enemy! You should be glad I'm doing your job for you!"

"Our job isn't to kill him. It's not even our job to punish him. We only want to arrest him, to turn him over to the proper authorities so that he can't hurt anyone else."

"He's already hurt me! I demand vengeance!" I cried.

"I can't permit vengeance," she said. "I can only promise you justice."

"Justice?" I said, as my computer brain fed me waves of wireless information. I instantly comprehended the American judicial system, and its pathetic inadequacies. "You think throwing him into a prison cell can ever fix the harm he's done to me?"

"No," said Mother Justice. "But letting victims seek their own revenge is a path to anarchy. We do what we must to preserve the common good."

"What does the common good of mankind matter to me?"

"You're an ant," said Mother Justice. "Of all the species on earth, yours should grasp the importance of selflessly acting for the good of all, rather than selfishly seeking to serve yourself. Humans and ants aren't all that different. We do our best when we work together."

"If I were still an ant, I might believe this," I said, feeling a wave of sorrow building beneath my still boiling rage. "But I'm a monster now, all alone, never to be reunited with my brothers. There can be no justice for me. Revenge is all that remains! Stand aside, or I'll scatter your molecules into the stratosphere!"

"Do what you must," said Mother Justice. "I won't stand aside."

I glowered at her, my anger building. Yet... there was something in her face. A look of calm resolution that unnerved me. Did she have some trick, some hidden power I was unaware of that might be capable of inflicting harm upon me?

To my surprise, she answered my unspoken question.

"I don't have the strength to harm you. If you choose to kill me to reach Dr. Mayhem, I can't stop you."

"You... you're telepathic," I said. "You're reading my thoughts."

"Yes," she said.

"I'm wondering why you aren't fleeing in terror, if you can see the rage within me."

"I see the pain within you," she said. "A pain that comes from loneliness. Just like in all the others."

"The others?" I asked.

"You aren't the first giant insect that Dr. Mayhem has brought into the world," said Mother Justice. "Or the first we've stopped from murdering him."

"By stopped, you mean you killed the other monsters," I said. While she could see into my thoughts, her thoughts were hidden from me. "You can't let something like me simply wander free in the world."

"We can," she said. "Admittedly, it's a somewhat small part of the world. There's an island in the Pacific that the

99

United Nations has transformed into a preserve where creatures like you can live in peace, far removed from mankind."

"A prison," I said.

"A home," she said. "Not all of Dr. Mayhem's creations have been as intelligent as you are. With the right leadership, the island might be transformed into a paradise."

"Now that you've told me of such a place, I can find it without your help," I said. "There's no reason I shouldn't go ahead and crush Dr. Mayhem's skull like a melon!"

"Please don't crush my skull like a melon," Dr. Mayhem whimpered.

Addressing him directly, I snarled, "You made me a monster! Now you beg me for mercy?"

Dr. Mayhem dropped to his knees, lifting his hands toward me. "Begging! Yes! I'm begging you!"

"I'm not begging," said Mother Justice. "I'm only clarifying your options. You can kill him and forever be the monster he wanted you to be. You can let him live and define your own identity. Dr. Mayhem might have created you, but only you can choose what to do with your life."

I contemplated my choices, searching through the collected online libraries of mankind, absorbing every digitized line of literature and philosophy in the time it took a tear to trace its way down Dr. Mayhem's cheek.

As I analyzed the wisdom of ages, I saw the uncomfortable truth. The fact that I'd been born meant I was now fated to die. Dr. Mayhem, too, would die, as would Mother Justice, as would the very planet I stood upon, one day, when a swollen sun consumed it in its final dying throws. In the Ozymandian vastness of time, whether I killed Dr. Mayhem mattered nothing at all.

"Are we truly born only to die?" I groaned.

"Welcome to the human condition, Bub," said Thundergun who was back on his feet, clutching his ribs. "Or the inhuman condition, in your case."

"Our time upon this world is finite," said Mother Justice. "Which means we must make the most of each moment granted to us. Do you want to live the remaining span of your life as a killer, or as a being capable of wisdom and mercy?"

I nodded slowly, weighing both paths.

"I shall spare him," I said to Mother Justice.

"I knew you would. As for getting you to the island, we can arrange—"

"There's no need," I said, rising into the air. "Your thoughts are hidden, but your companions are open books. I see the location of the island in their minds. I can travel there under my own power."

I glanced at Thundergun and Hummingbird, both of them battered and bloodied. I saw their broken bones and internal injuries caused by my attack. With all the medical knowledge of humanity flowing into me, I used my telekinesis to knit their bones, muscles and blood vessels back into proper order.

"Safe journey," said Mother Justice. "I hope you'll no longer feel alone once you reach the island!"

"Loneliness is my destiny," I said to her as I hovered over the destroyed roof. "But, with my fellow atomic insects, perhaps there will be comfort in being alone, together."

I turned my faceted eyes toward the west, seeing the distant Pacific in my mind's eye. The wind roared across my carapace as I soared toward infinite possible futures.

The Itsy, Bitsy Spider

THE ITSY, BITSY SPIDER

LENA NG

There were a lot of things eight-year-old Tara didn't like. She didn't like her five-year-old little brother, Thomas. "Go away," she said whenever he appeared whether she was cutting out paper dolls or coloring in her book or building lock block houses. "Stop bugging me." She was a big girl and couldn't be bothered by little brothers.

She didn't like insects. Not crawly black beetles. Not fuzzy bumblebees who enjoyed a good buzz. Not even black-spotted lady bugs or green, chirpy crickets or ambling caterpillars who would grow up to be lovely butterflies.

And she certainly, most definitely, absolutely positively didn't like spiders, all fat, hairy bodies and scurrying legs. Any time Tara saw one, even though her mom and dad told her to leave it alone, she'd bend her knee, raise up her foot and—

squash

—be done with it. It might be minding its own business, catching flies. It might be spinning delicate, complicated webs with its own home-made silk, its thread as strong as steel. It could be doing an eight-legged tap dance wearing four pairs of tiny, shiny shoes. Did any of that impress Tara? No. Tara just had to see one and—

squash

It would be a splotch on the pavement. Or a smoosh on the wall. Or a smear in the corner.

Yes, some spiders can be dangerous. Yes, some spiders can be venomous with a wicked bite. Yes, some spiders can pop out of a cupboard and look at you with their eight beady, black eyes.

But Tara didn't live in a place where the spiders were big or angry or venomous. She just didn't like a lot of things.

One day, Tara was on her way to the playground. She skipped over all the sidewalk cracks. She tangled through a random skipping rope. She stuck a tongue at Mrs. Langhorne's old and yappy, fuzzy-haired Pomeranian. As she turned down the street, an eight-legged, minding-its-own-business, not-causing-anyone-problems spider strolled across the sidewalk. An itsy, bitsy spider the size of a marble. It looked at Tara with all eight of its black, beady eyes and said, "Hello there!"

Tara heard it, bent her knee, raised up her foot and—
squash

And that was the end of the spider. A miracle of a talking spider, now a squish on the sidewalk.

Tara strolled on her way. She hop-scotched over Mr. Chang's yard. She swatted Mrs. Johnson's bird-feeder. She climbed over Mr. Singh's fence. As she yanked a tulip from Mrs. Garcia's garden, an eight-legged, fuzzy-bellied spider, the size of a baseball popped out from under the bushes. "Hello," it said, in a tinny, worried voice. "Have you seen my little brother?"

Tara heard it, bent her knee, raised up her foot and—
squash

And that was the end of the spider. A miracle of a talking spider, now a splotch by the bushes.

Tara power-walked on her way. Where were all these spiders coming from? She was getting rather worried. She hurried through Mr. Ladipo's hedges. She yanked on Mrs. Bannon's oak tree branches. She rushed through Mr. Dawson's backyard. Her trip to the playground seemed to take much longer than usual. As she squeezed through Mrs. Olsen's fence, an eight-legged, fuzzy-faced spider, the size of a puppy, bounded out from under a car. "Hey," it said, in a squeaky, worried voice. "Have you seen my little sister?"

Tara heard it, bent her knee, raised up her foot and—

squash

And that was the end of the spider. A miracle of a talking spider, now a smear on the pavement.

Tara dashed on her way. She was becoming awfully afraid. She sprinted through Mr. Lao's yard. She tore through Mrs. Wolak's hanging laundry. She raced by Mr. Peterson's RV. As she galloped by Mrs. Rudnik's house, an eight-legged spider, as big as an elephant, stepped in front of the way. She clacked her fangs and asked in a deep, spine-tingling voice, "Hey, have you seen my children?"

Tara didn't answer, but she did drool a little.

Mama Spider saw the squish on the sidewalk. She saw the splotch by the bushes. She saw the smear on the pavement. She bent her knee, raised a big, fat, hairy leg and—

SQUASH!

And that was the end of Tara.

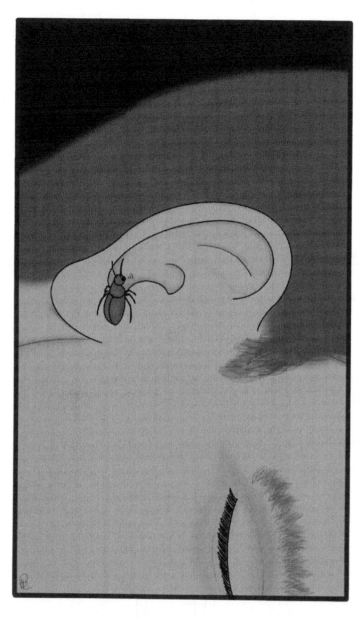

Dr. Optera's Intelligent Bugs

DR. OPTERA'S INTELLIGENT BUGS

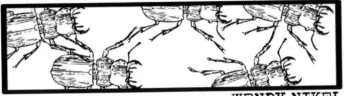

WENDY NIKEL

Dr. Cole Optera leaned in toward the tiny, six-legged creature. Its unblinking eyes stared back at him. "Come on," he whispered. "Say something."

The creature sat silently. Its leg twitched. Not precisely the sign of intelligence he'd been hoping for, not after all the time and effort. Not after all the ridicule.

Optera sighed and set the beetle back in its enclosure. There was still something wrong with his methods... some factor he wasn't considering. He rubbed his head. He squeezed his eyes shut, trying to concentrate. When he opened them, he caught sight of the digital clock, its bright red numbers chastising him for being up so late, for skipping dinner (again), and for drinking too much coffee past sundown.

Resignedly, Optera stumbled to the hotel room bed and threw himself upon it, still fully clothed in the slacks and button-down shirt he'd donned so many hours ago for his conference presentation. He flicked the light off on the beetle sitting perfectly still in its enclosure.

If he'd stayed awake a moment longer to tidy up his workstation, then he might have heard the bug, with a voice no louder than a whisper, say "Hello?"

If he'd have paused for another moment to double-check the lid on the beetle's enclosure, none of it might have happened.

Scuffle, scuffle.
Sleek, smooth glass. Climbing, crawling. Upward.
Scuffle, scuffle.
Downward.
Scuffle, scuffle.
Carpet. Cleaning solution, harsh and sharp.
Scuffle, scuffle.
A door, closed. Squeeze under through the tiny space. Freeze in the shock of bright light.
Scuffle, scuffle.
Frantic crawling. Under again. Back into the dark.
A noise. A being. Breathing.
Scuffle, scuffle.
Up the woven cloth. Closer to the noise.
Scuffle, scuffle.
A head. A face. An earlobe. Concentrate, form the words.
"Feeeeeeed. Meeeee."

Across the hall from Dr. Optera's room, Dr. Jennifer Lorenz woke with a start. She scratched her ear and rolled over, but her mind was already awake with that awful, nagging feeling that she'd forgotten something... something very important.

"Food?" she muttered to herself. Why was she thinking of food? Did she forget to have dinner again? These conferences were always a bit hit or miss with the meals. She'd spend far too much time trying to catch the eye of a generous donor or the attention of an expert in her field, and by the time she made it to the buffet table, the caterers would already be cleaning up.

But no, she had eaten today. She'd ordered a burger in the bar downstairs afterward while she talked with that crazy lunatic scientist, the one who was trying to teach his beetles how to talk. After finishing her burger, she'd wrapped up the fries in a napkin and made some excuse, anything to get away from his ravings. These kind of conferences always brought out the weird ones.

And yet… there was something about food.

Unable to remain still, she sat up in her bed and leaned over to the nightstand where she'd kept her purse. She never liked to leave it too far away in strange places like this. The zipper stuck, but she managed to pry it open and took out the napkin-wrapped fries. For some reason just having them out of her purse, sitting on the nightstand, made her feel more settled. Obviously, she must have simply been worried that she'd forget them, like that apple she'd put in there once and forgotten about until it was nothing but a pile of mush in the bottom.

She clicked off the light, yawned, and rolled over. With the peaceful satisfaction that she'd remembered something very important, she drifted back off to sleep.

Scuffle, scuffle.
The rooms are full of food for us.
Scuffle, scuffle.
They give us all we need.
Scuffle, scuffle.
Wait in the day, tucked into the mattresses' layers.
Scuffle, scuffle.
Tonight, we talk. Tomorrow, we feast again.

Optera couldn't sleep. He had new beetles shipped to the hotel room overnight, but when he came back from his shower, they – like the others – were gone. He spent the evening tearing apart the room, combing the carpet to discover how they'd escape. This conference was going to be a complete bust without at least something to show the others during his final presentation. He'd have preferred to have his original beetles, but even brand-new ones would do for demonstrating his methods. He certainly couldn't demonstrate with an empty cage.

He needed more beetles, and he needed them fast.

Unfortunately, it seemed that his only solution was to beg for some off that worthless Dr. Pitterknuckle, the only other scientist he knew of that would have brought beetles to the conference.

"Can I help you, Dr. Optera?" The clerk, Jillian, asked as he leaned over the front desk.

"Yes. I need to know the room number for a Dr. Pitterknuckle."

"Room 153, sir."

"Thank you." Optera turned to leave, but as he did, he noted a plated sandwich at his feet.

"What is this?"

"Is what?"

"This sandwich. Did you put that there?"

"Why, yes. I'm feeding the hungry."

"What hungry?"

"Well, the hungry." Jillian screwed up her face. "Bugs, perhaps. Yes. They need food, too, don't they?"

"Well, how do you know they're hungry? Do you always leave food out for them?"

"Recently."

"Why?"

"I... I just know," Jillian said, shrugging. "Doesn't everyone leave food out for the bugs? It's the sympathetic thing to do. Humane."

"Where did you hear that? In school? On TV? On the news?"

"Well, no. I don't rightly recall."

Optera frowned as he made his way down the corridor to room 153. At each of the doorways sat a plate or napkin, on which rested some sort of food. "What is wrong with these people?" he muttered under his breath, though he had a sinking feeling he might already know.

Reaching room 153, he knocked on Pitterknuckle's door.

The man who answered was thick and red-faced, with a carefully trimmed, white beard. Optera had often wondered if, during the holiday season, children mistook him for Santa.

"What do you want, Optera?" he bellowed.

"I... I was wondering if I might borrow some of your beetles for tomorrow's presentation. Mine seem to have gone missing. I thought I might offer to buy you lunch today to compensate." He glanced over his colleague's shoulder. "Oh, never mind. I see you've already ordered room service."

"I did?" Pitterknuckle turned around and stared in awe at the mounding plate of food on the table. "Oh. I suppose I did. No, actually, that's not for me."

"I'm sorry," Optera said. "Were you expecting company?"

Pitterknuckle scratched his beard and then turned a brighter shade of red as though remembering something embarrassing. "It's for the bugs."

"The bugs? Your bugs you mean?"

"Sure. Bugs have to eat, too." He nudged Optera into the hall and pulled the door shut behind him. "Come on, let's go down to lunch."

Scuffle, scuffle.
We reproduce faster when we're so well-fed.
Scuffle, scuffle.
It's time to move to bigger pastures.
Scuffle, scuffle.
Tagalong creatures in bellhop's pockets and maid's creaking carts.
Scuffle, scuffle.
Let us feast, and feast some more.

Dr. Optera sat at a bar stool, staring at his drink.

Before him, the barkeeper had mounded up piles of crackers and hot wings and potato crisps and burgers. In fact, every kind of food that the restaurant served was also laid out on the table. Optera, misinterpreting this generosity, had reached for a fry, only to be scolded by the barkeeper.

"Oy! That's not for you, man! Feeding the less fortunate, here!"

The 'less fortunate' refused to show their beady, bug-eyed faces, nor would they answer when Optera ran through the hallways, calling out to them, begging for them to see reason. The other guests had heard, of course, and threatened to call the authorities.

"Those little monsters." Optera slammed down his drink. "They're abusing the powers I gave them!"

A woman who'd been sitting two bar stools down took one look at him, picked up her drink, and found a different table.

But how else could they be staging this coup? They must be doing something to turn this hotel into a landfill of half-eaten food. There had to be a way to correct this imbalance.

"Hey, weren't you talking with that pretty scientist last time you were in here?" the barkeeper asked. "I take it that didn't work out?"

"Who? Dr. Lorenz? Oh, no. We aren't together. She's just a colleague. She studies…"

"What?" the barkeeper asked. "What does she study?"

Optera threw back the last of his drink, placed a few dollars on the table atop some egg rolls, and raced from the bar.

Scuffle. Rest.
Lazy and well-fed, the food now comes to us.
They do just what we say.
With their malleable minds and their unending stores of food.
This is the life we deserve.
Resting, eating, rest some more.
We didn't even hear them coming.
The terrible creatures with their too-many legs.
They spun their webs among us.

Initially, Dr. Lorenz wished that that crazy Optera hadn't included her in his presentation. After all, she wouldn't want anyone to think that she had anything to do with that insane experiment of his, even if she did provide the solution that put an end to the beetle's feeding frenzy.

"I believe," he said at his entomology talk (the most well-attended one he'd ever given) "that the beetles, with their new understanding of human language, were using it to their advantage. The sleeping mind is quite open to suggestion, and the beetles somehow knew this. Their desire to be fed was perhaps simple, but left the ecosystem unbalanced. Therefore, I had to restore the balance using their natural predators."

His speech did receive a standing ovation, though, particularly from the hotel owners. They only now, it seemed, realized what a disaster it would have been had the health inspectors found out. After the speech, Dr. Optera brought her the carefully packaged box containing her spiders.

"I couldn't have done it without you, you know. They were quite effective hunters. A toast," Dr. Optera declared, holding up a glass of champagne, "to Dr. Lorenz and her spiders."

Well, maybe he isn't all that bad, she thought as the crowd clapped politely for her. Her dislike for him softened even more when the conference director asked her to be next year's guest of honor, and it disappeared entirely when a rich investor offered to fund her next twelve months of study.

Back in her hotel room, after a glorious evening of basking in complements and praise, Dr. Lorenz double-checked her pillow for bugs. She lay down, and – exhausted from the exciting, unexpected events of the day – she closed her eyes and allowed herself sleep.

If she'd stayed awake a moment longer to tidy up her workstation, then she might have noticed the spiders, with a coordinated effort that was most un-spiderlike, spin a web resembling a ladder up the edge of the enclosure.

If she'd have paused for another moment to double-check the lid on the spiders' enclosure, none of it might have happened.

Scuffle, scuffle.
With the words of the two-leggeds, we negotiated.
We will uphold our end of the bargain.
Six-legged and eight-legged together.
In time, the world will be ours.

JACK AND THE BED BUGS

WILLIAM SHAW

It was raining in Jack's garden, which could mean only one thing: the giant was hanging out his laundry. Ever since that misunderstanding with the beanstalk and the goose with golden eggs, Jack's neighbor Gerald had delighted in such petty domestic annoyances, blasting his self-playing harp in the middle of the night and dumping his rubbish down Jack's chimney. If Jack complained, Gerald would look at him as if he'd forgotten he was there, and say "Oh hello, Jack. I was just thinking about talking to the police about that attempted burglary. What do you think?" and Jack would be forced to drop it.

By now, Jack was used to grinning and bearing it as second-hand soapy water cascaded onto his garden. But when a giant brown insect landed on his lawn, he had to admit this was something different. And when the giant brown insect was joined by two, three, four, ten more giant brown insects, which swiftly began devouring his vegetable patch, he realized this was an entirely new form of revenge.

The giant bed bugs did not respond to traditional treatment. Jack tried spraying them with peppermint oil, but they just swarmed his pantry and carried away his stores of mint imperials. He tried using bleach to ward them off, but he only ended up dying his lawn blonde. He tried fumigation, but the pesticides which worked on regular bed bugs only made these ones bigger and nastier. They soon went from stealing mint imperials to stealing flour and apples, and eventually graduated to active antisocial behavior. One morning Jack woke up to find that his garden shed had been dismantled and rebuilt into a statue of a giant bed bug, pointing at Jack's house and laughing. This was the final straw, and Jack found himself climbing the beanstalk to Gerald's house that very afternoon.

Gerald lived in a fashionable bungalow nestled between the clouds, and Jack had to make another lengthy climb just to ring the doorbell. On his last visit he'd managed to slip in through the disused cat flap, but that had been nailed shut by now, and anyway, he needed to make a good impression this time. When Gerald finally answered the door, and finished laughing at Jack hanging limply off the doorbell, he carried Jack in and deposited him on the kitchen table.

"Well then, young Jack," said Gerald. "What can I do for you, my boy?"

Jack was not a boy any more — he had turned eighteen just a few months ago — but he let the comment slide. He had to play nicely if he wanted rid of those bugs.

"Well," said Jack. "The other day you dropped some bed bugs on my land..."

"Did I really?" asked Gerald, barely suppressing a smirk. "That is most unfortunate."

"Yes, well, I was wondering if you could help me get rid of them," said Jack.

"No can do, I'm afraid," Gerald replied. "Goes against the Giant County Bylaws. Any and all giant livestock ceases to be my property once it leaves my airspace. Once they're on your land, they're your responsibility. Nothing to do with me."

Jack crumpled. "But can't you even—"

"No," said Gerald. "Those bugs are your problem, and that's flat. Now if you'll excuse me, I need to take these golden eggs to market before they get cold." He gestured at a basket full of fresh golden eggs, each of them about half the size of one of Jack's bed bugs.

"But can't you at least tell me how to get rid of them?" demanded Jack. "None of the normal methods work!"

"Hmm," said Gerald, stroking his chin as he basked in Jack's misery. "Well, normally I just dose them with a bit of liquid fat and protein. Clears them right up. But I don't suppose you'd know where to get that?"

"No," admitted Jack. "But I know somebody who might."

"Well well well," said Bessie. "Look who's come crawling back."

Bessie had come a long way since Jack first traded her for some magic beans all those years ago. Having witnessed a classic example of bad contract negotiation, she had built a successful career as a commercial lawyer, and now helped negotiate deals for several major corporations. She was by far the cleverest person Jack knew, even if she was a cow. If anyone could help him right now, it was her.

"Let me get this straight," said Bessie. "You're dealing with a giant bed bug infestation, dumped on you by your giant neighbor, and you need my help finding a pesticide?"

"That's right," said Jack.

"OK then," Bessie sighed. "What is this pesticide?"

"Gerald said he used liquid fat and protein to kill them. Do you know where I could get some of that?"

Bessie blinked, then stared at Jack over her spectacles, as if she was wondering if he was serious.

"Liquid fat and protein? Dear boy, that's milk. He told you to spray them with milk?"

Jack shrugged. "He said it works for him. And don't call me boy, please. I turned eighteen three months ago."

"Well, I don't know much about pest control," said Bessie. "But I do know about the art of the deal. You can have the usage rights to my milk, but only if I get a 50% cut of any profits from the endeavor and the right to cease the contract at any time."

"Um," said Jack. "Alright then."

"Splendid," said Bessie, thrusting out a hoof which Jack gingerly shook. "The milk will arrive in five working days."

Five working days later, Jack prepared to disinfect his land. Bessie's milk had been poured into a large tank, which was now strapped to Jack's back. He was going to spray his garden with it, and hopefully get rid of those bed bugs once and for all. Bessie had come round to supervise the use of her milk, and ensure the operation was conducted in the spirit of fair dealing. Jack just wanted the whole thing over with.

Jack stepped cautiously into the garden, staggering slightly under the weight of Bessie's milk. The first thing he saw was a bed bug, snacking idly on one of his garden gnomes. Jack lifted up his spray tool and gave a cautious squirt, and a jet of white liquid caught the bed bug full in the face. Then something very strange happened.

The bed bug gave a short, groaning wheeze, and keeled over onto its back. A weird sizzling sound filled the air, and before Jack and Bessie knew what was happening, the bed bug's body had turned completely into sun-drenched gold. Jack gave it a small kick, and swore as the hard metal hurt his foot. Bessie approached the bed bug more cautiously, and gave it an experimental lick.

"No doubt about it," said Bessie. "This bed bug is solid gold."

Jack gaped at the dead, shining pest. Solid gold! If all the bed bugs did this after being sprayed with Bessie's milk... they were rich! Even richer than Gerald, whose golden eggs were barely half the size of a single dead bed bug! Jack shot Bessie a grin, and began spraying in earnest.

Jack and Bessie had had a tiring day. After a hard morning spraying Jack's garden with milk, they had spent a long afternoon loading the heavy gold bed bugs into Jack's cart, ready to take to market the next day. (All profits would be split between them 50-50, as stipulated in Bessie's contract). They were just admiring their new treasures when the ground started shaking beneath them.

Looking up, the pair saw a pop-eyed and red-faced Gerald striding towards the house. Gerald was not very genial at the best of times, but in this moment it was clear he was not a happy giant.

"What do you think you're doing?" he bellowed, making the window panes in Jack's house rattle. "Those bed bugs came from my bed sheets! You can't go carting them off to market! You'll undercut my golden eggs!"

"Ahem," said Bessie, and Jack recognized the face that usually preceded a lecture on legal proceedings.

"Hang on Bessie, I'll handle this," said Jack. He turned to face the giant.

"Look Gerald," said Jack. "According to the Giant County Bylaws, any and all giant livestock ceases to be yours once it leaves your airspace. Once the bed bugs are on my land, they become my responsibility."

"But they're mine!" shouted Gerald. "Mine boy, do you hear me?"

"I'm afraid not," said Jack. "You said it yourself: these bed bugs are my property, and that's flat. They've got nothing to do with you. And don't call me boy, please. I'm eighteen years old."

Gerald could do nothing but stand there and splutter as Jack and Bessie hopped up onto the cart.

"Now if you'll excuse me," said Jack. "My business partner and I need to transport these bed bugs to a secure storage location before market day tomorrow."

Gerald was speechless as Jack and Bessie set off into the evening light. Even so, Jack couldn't help but call back:

"May the best gold-seller win!"

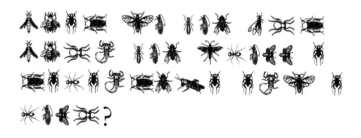

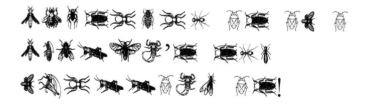

STREAK

R. C. CAPASSO

he storm is breaking up. You should be able to fly in an hour, when the winds drop." Rafael turned to study Kash. "Are you ready?"

"Of course." Kash made his voice as hearty as he could. "I was born for this."

Since he was short and scrawny, that much seemed true. You can't be tall or beefy and ride a mosquito.

Rafael nodded. If he had doubts about Kash's plan, he was nice enough to hide them.

Kash would have felt sick to his stomach if Rafael had doubted him. Rafael was his hero. Actually, he was everyone's hero. The first to capture and train a dragonfly to accept a human rider. The first to start a herd, breeding them to hunt the most dangerous giant insects like the tsetse fly. Somewhere Rafael had a small box holding the Kelsinger Medal for Service to Humanity. The medal showed a rising sun over raging seas.

The initial cataclysmic floods happened before Kash was born, but he'd heard all about them. Cities destroyed, habitats altered. Swampland and bayous formed as climate change altered coastlands, driving water far inland. And the water wasn't the only disaster. Humanity realized too late that all the illegal dumping in oceans and lakes bred a toxic tide. People got sick, fish died, and insects began to grow.

121

Nightmarishly big and lethal. It took only one human generation, thousands of insect generations, for the world to be overrun—over flown—with buzzing, stinging, gnawing creatures.

"Hey." Sarai broke into Kash's thoughts. She wore a bright yellow slicker and her short-cropped black hair peeked out from under a ball cap. "The mini-blimp's emptied out. I should be able to hold a dozen people."

Kash stood and nodded. For Sarai he'd like to be six foot and built like a pro wrestler. Assuming that's what she'd like. Of course, he'd never know what she liked because he couldn't string two coherent words together in her presence. She was sixteen, his age, but somehow she had her life together. She was smart, pretty and brave. When he came up with the plan, she'd signed on at once.

"Is Streak ready?" Rafael strode to the thick-plated glass overlooking the hangar he'd constructed.

A dozen large solar lamps illuminated the airy space, softened by living green walls. Kash came to stand beside Rafael, looking down. His steed, a sleek female mosquito, moved her fine antennae. Just over five feet to the thorax, with a wingspan of about twenty feet, she was a medium size for the new strains. All she needed was a halter and saddle.

"Ready."

"Winds are down." Rafael moved to the desk that held radar, maps, and radio. He stared out a large window into the night sky. "Now take it easy. Keep in radio contact. "I…" Rafael paused. "I'll send help if you need it."

Rafael was 26. Too long in leg and broad in shoulder to be a mosquito ace. He could barely ride a few minutes on the fattest of houseflies. He hated to stay on the ground, but he didn't waste time on his ego. He'd poured all his knowledge into Kash, knowing the world needed people small enough and brave enough to be insect jockeys.

Kash pounded down the stairs and strode up to his mosquito. With a blue gleaming exoskeleton touched with white dots, she was one of the more beautiful of the species, if you could get past the threatening proboscis, the black compound eyes and the waving antennae. Kash had learned not to judge by looks; he wasn't exactly handsome himself. But he knew he was in the minority. Most humans fled the approach of any of the giant insects, and they had a history of horror to justify them.

There were still a lot of questions about the mutant insects, like how much bigger they might get, how intelligent they were and if, with their multiplied size, they might also live longer than the original species. At one time, when they were still tiny, female mosquitoes with adequate food supply might live five months. Streak had been with Kash for nine months now and showed no signs of weakening.

Streak tilted a feeler toward Kash, and he let it brush his face. It hadn't been easy to train her, but now she responded readily to him, allowing him approach to feed her with buckets of the non-blood protein fluid he and Rafael had concocted. She took to the saddle and even apparently enjoyed his occasional touch. Streak would never be warm or beautiful like a horse, but through her Kash owned the skies. He'd make the most of every day, every mission on her back.

Kash tightened the cinch, slipped his foot into the stirrup and swung his body onto Streak's thorax. He gave a quick nod to Rafael as Raf powered the huge bay doors open. He lightly touched the reins.

"Go."

A few steps out of the hangar and the giant insect paused an instant in the fresh air. Pulsing lights above them indicated that massive fireflies were emerging after the storm. Nocturnal insects of all kinds would be moving again, drawn by the moisture and warmth. Streak's wings quivered for a moment, then gave a mighty pulse. Kash caught his breath, excitement shooting through his body. This never got old, the lift off the earth, the rush of air against him. The power and freedom.

"Seek!" he shouted against the creature's head.

Oblivious to the dark, Streak shot forward.

Kash sent a quick look down to the hangar. The floodwaters roiled maybe a quarter of a mile away, but Rafael had built on the clearing of a hill; their ranch wouldn't be damaged. Behind him he watched as a white shape, like a mushroom cap circled with light, grew and slowly rose. Sarai's mini-blimp, ringed with solar lamps, had taken off. Already Streak was leaving them behind, but the radio crackled.

"I'm up, Kash."

"I see you." Somehow he could talk when he was airborne. Maybe it was the strength of Streak under him or the sense of mission. Or not looking into Sarai's big brown eyes. Whatever the cause, he'd welcomed every training exercise, every dry run. "Heading north."

Dependent on a small motor and the wind, Sarai's blimp would be slower. But once Kash reached his goal, she wouldn't be far behind.

"Seek!" he repeated to Streak.

The mosquito was already turning.

"There!" Kash shouted, then waved his arm, knowing Sarai would never hear him.

Deep in the valley a family crouched on the roof of their house. Floodwaters washed against the second-story windows and sprayed up over the eaves. They waved flashlights, signaling for help. But when the dim lights reflected off Streak's reddish abdomen, they started screaming. One woman broke from the group, clutching her hair, running to the edge of the roof. She stopped at the edge, one foot moving forward. Ready to plunge into the flood.

Kash pulled hard on Streak's reins. Obedient, Streak beat her wings and shot upward into the dark. Kash gripped the saddle horn, flattening himself against the sudden ascent.

The woman would rather drown than be stabbed and bled by a massive mosquito. Kash couldn't blame her. No one would ever forget the early attacks, the images sent round the world.

But Sarai's blimp flew into sight. Already her voice fought the wind, calling down through her loud speaker, reassuring, encouraging, shouting instructions. As her craft centered over the house, she sent down the rescue basket. The survivors caught the basket, grabbed the children and lifted them in first. Even the frantic woman turned, her face lifted in hope. She edged back along the roof toward Sarai.

Kash and Streak hovered out of sight as the last of the family ascended toward the blimp. Kash could barely believe the plan had worked.

Female mosquitoes are masters at finding human bodies, detecting their heat, skin odor and the carbon dioxide emissions. Kash was the only one to ever think that this power could be used for something good. Like finding survivors in storms, floods, and landslides where overwhelmed military, police and emergency workers couldn't go. Only Sarai believed in his plan enough to fly the rescue ship.

He counted six people clinging together in the blimp's gondola.

"Room for six or seven more," Sarai radioed.

Kash leaned forward and stroked Streak's scaly head. The creature might not have iridescent wings like a dragonfly or give light like a firefly. But she had something to offer. And so did Kash. If he ever grew too heavy to ride, he'd train more mosquitoes and teach more riders. He'd share every idea that came into his head. Maybe scientists could learn something from the insects. How did they process the toxic waters and grow instead of dying?

But for the moment he had a mission. "Come on, girl. Seek."

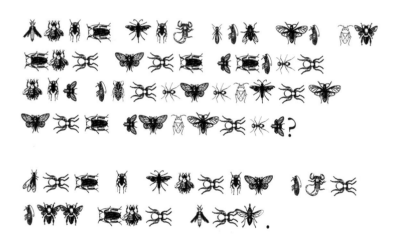

LOVEBUGS BITE

SONJA THOMAS

Bug off, Lovebug!" I bark.

My little brother's face crumbles and in three... two... one... he tears off down the hall screaming, "Mom! Becky's being mean to me!"

Usually, I'd follow him to defend my case and avoid punishment. Instead, I return to staring out the window, waiting for my ride to Keenan's birthday party.

The nickname Lovebug may sound "adorable" and "endearing" (Mom's words, not mine), but it's perfect. Because even though the species of March flies that folks in the south call lovebugs don't sting or bite and they're not poisonous—technically they're not even bugs—they're also loathed by most people for being a pest. Especially this time of year when they're everywhere.

Now, don't think of me as a hater. I love lovebugs. In fact, I love all bugs. And I guess I love my brother too, although I'd never let him hear me say it.

Finally, Mrs. Schott's SUV pulls into the driveway.

"Bye, Mom!" I call over my shoulder and bolt out the front door. I slide into the backseat next to my best friend Ash. He lifts his chin and we bump fists.

"Thanks for the ride, Mrs. Schott."

She smiles at me in the rearview mirror before pulling out of the driveway.

Sitting in the passenger seat is my other best friend, and Mrs. Schott's mini-clone, Missy. "Did you guys see the Marlins crush the Nats last night?" she asks.

Ash and Missy launch into a heated debate over a baseball game. Sports aren't my thing, so I watch the palm trees blur as we speed down the highway, heading toward the park. The car slows to a stop at a red light, right next to a van with the company name, "Bug Be Gone." Underneath is a cartoon ant lying on its back with Xs for eyes and the slogan, "The Bug Stops Here."

I shake my head in disgust.

"People don't seem to get that killing bugs also kills our planet."

"Uh-oh," Ash smirks, "we're about to get schooled by the bug expert."

Missy covers her mouth, unsuccessfully suppressing her giggles.

"Bees are dying because of pesticides. I don't know why they won't use some natural, nontoxic stuff to keep insects from annoying humans." I snarl at the Bug Be Gone van as it zooms away from the light. "No bees mean no almonds, no peaches, and no chocolate."

"No chocolate?" Mrs. Schott blurts. "Nope, can't have that now, can we."

Splat-splat-splat!

"Then again," she mutters. White smears stain the windshield. "I hate lovebugs."

As a future entomologist—a scientist who studies insects—I can't agree with her. Having access to all the creepy, crawly critters in Florida is pretty fly!

"Interesting fact," I say, my body bouncing with excitement. "Baby lovebugs eat decomposing animals and plants. Then they put essential nutrients back into the ground. So lovebugs are like an organic recycling system!"

Missy wrinkles her nose. "Yuck."

I sigh. No one appreciates the benefits of bugs.

"Hey!" Ash taps his finger on his window. "What is that?"

"A blackbird?" Missy suggests.

"I don't think so." Ash yanks out his cell and starts filming. "More like a UFC."

"Ultimate Fighting Champion?" I ask.

Missy snorts.

"No," Ash replies, never taking his eyes off his phone. "An unidentified flying creature."

I'm twisting my head trying to get a look at this so-called UFC, when the car makes a sharp turn and bumps along a gravel drive into the park's parking lot. A huge pavilion decorated with balloons and streamers houses a large crowd. In the center, I spot Keenan sporting a birthday crown.

Missy, Ash, and I pile out of the air-conditioned car. The hot August sun instantly warms my skin.

Dead lovebugs cover the SUV's front bumper. I want to share that the bugs' guts are acidic and if they bake too long in the sun it'll burn through the paint. But Mrs. Schott probably knows this since lovebugs swarm for a few weeks every spring and summer. I head toward the party instead.

"Have fun kids." Mrs. Schott waves as she drives off.

Ash hasn't moved, still staring at his phone. "This is no bird."

"C'mon, guys." Missy pulls on Ash's arm. "They're starting to play water tag!"

My two friends race towards the pavilion. I look up into the sky. No clouds. No birds. No UFCs. Nothing. Whatever Ash saw is gone. I shrug and join my friends who are sitting on one of the wooden benches.

"We have to wait." Missy pouts. "There's only ten super soakers and vests."

Keenan's father strolls up to the pavilion carrying a huge basket and calls out, "Harvey's Grove next door donated a bunch of fruit for the party, including these sweet-smelling Honeybells!"

"Hey, Mr. Smith!" Ash says, holding up both hands open wide. "Toss me one of those, please." Mr. Smith throws one over and, just like when he's in left field, Ash easily catches the baseball-sized orange.

Keenan's father hands both Missy and me a Honeybell. I slip mine into my pocket.

"Stupid bloodsucking skeeters." Ash slaps his left arm, then lifts his hand exposing a smooshed mosquito.

I spare the lecture on their benefits—like pollination and protecting the rainforest—and light a citronella candle on a nearby picnic table instead. Ash happily munches on his orange, oblivious to my warding off future bloodsuckers without resorting to murder.

We watch as Keenan dodges a shot of water from his younger sister Kelly and takes cover behind a barricade. After a few moments, Keenan doubles back, steadily pumping his water gun. He blasts Kelly and two other kids with a super long stream, at least twenty feet.

I nudge Ash's shoulder. "Can I see that UFC video?"

He cues it up. I take his phone and hit play. There is something unrecognizable in the sky. My eyes narrow, inspecting the shaky feed. Black. Branching wings. Almost the size of a small blackbird, but Ash was right. This is no bird.

I watch the video again, then pause and zoom in. There's a tiny head in front of the reddish-orange humpback on its thorax. Short antennas. No stinger.

I zoom out for a clearer picture. Six, no, twelve legs and…
two heads on either end! That's the real giveaway: two flies
attached—one with bigger googly eyes than the other. Like
every other mating season, only much bigger.

I gasp.

"What?" Missy and Ash ask in unison.

"I think the UFCs are super-sized lovebugs!"

Ash's thick brows squish together. "Say what now?"

Before I can answer, a large shadow slowly moves over
the party. Staring up at the sky, my eyebrows shoot up.

I glance at Ash and Missy. Both are on their feet, their
mouths open wide. Most guests continue gabbing, eating, or
playing. A few people notice the small cluster of UFCs
overhead and point. Others whip out their phone to capture
the unusual sight.

The flying creatures ping-pong off one another, bouncing
around like a pinball game. They're too small to be birds. And
too big to be flies. But once I spot several of them stuck
together in flight, along with their bright red middle sections,
I'm now one hundred percent convinced.

"They *are* gigantic lovebugs."

Suddenly, the sky darkens. Hundreds, thousands, no, tens
of thousands of colossal lovebugs swarm overhead. The
flapping and fluttering from velvety black wings rings in my
ears. The water tag game freezes. Chaos follows.

Guests shriek. Kids bawl. A few adults pray. People run
around searching for loved ones. Some join us under the
shelter, huddled in fear. Many scramble to their cars. Horns
blare. Drivers shout. Cars idle, stuck in a parking lot traffic
jam.

Are we gonna survive this bug-apocalypse? Will I ever see
my mom and baby brother again?

Ash's phone vibrates in my hand and a high-pitched screech sounds. The harsh, grating noise from every nearby cell surrounds us. Ash snatches his phone back and we silently read the screen:

EMERGENCY ALERT:

THIS IS NOT A TEST. This is a message from the Federal Emergency Management Agency. There is a slow-moving flock of unusually large lovebugs confirmed in the following southern states: Texas, Louisiana, Mississippi, Alabama, Florida, Georgia, and South Carolina. All residents in these areas please take shelter and remain inside with all doors and windows closed until notified otherwise. Residents are asked to remain calm and not panic.

Almost everyone scatters from the pavilion toward the parking lot.

"You were right, Becky," Ash says.

Nausea grips me. I don't want to be right.

Ash picks at his afro. Missy hugs her stomach. "Should we hitch a ride home?"

I shake my head. "NO!"

"WHY?" Ash and Missy cry in unison.

"Heat attracts lovebugs. And exhaust fumes because they confuse the smell with decomposing plants. That's why they're always around highways."

A sudden realization hits. "With all these running engines, these mega-bugs will come straight at us!"

The three of us run to the parking lot, waving our arms, and yelling for everyone to turn off their cars. But with all the honking and arguing between drivers, the adults ignore our warnings.

"This isn't working," Missy cries. "Let me call my mom." She dials, huffs, and frantically tries again.

"Anything?" my voice cracks.

Missy shakes her head. "The phone lines are jammed."

"I can't reach my parents either," Ash says.

Missy looks at her phone again. "What if she's hurt? What if..." She starts to tremble. Her voice falls to a whisper. "I want to go home."

"How?" Ash says.

My body grows stiff. I want to say that everything will be alright, but that feels like a big fat lie. I also want to flee screaming.

"Becky, what do we do?" Missy pleads.

I stare at my scuffed sneakers.

"I don't know."

"But you're the bug expert!"

She's right. Taking a deep breath, I push aside my dizzying fear. I pace along the edge of the parking lot talking over everything I know about lovebugs.

"They're active during the day and stop flying at dusk. They hate wind, insect spray, wet surfaces, and citrus smells."

I pause, watching the horde sweep toward the main road. Just then a cluster breaks off and heads straight for the idling cars in the parking lot. They hover over the warmth from the running engines. An engine revs and the car smashes into another. I wince at the sound of crunched metal.

"Leave us alone!" Ash cries at the never-ending plague of insects. He runs back to the pavilion, snatches up an orange, and rushes back. "Suck on citrus!"

"Wait!" I lunge to stop him, but I'm too late.

Ash launches his citrus bomb at the rabble of bugs. Of course, he hits his target because my friend has mad pitching skills. A giant lovebug nosedives onto a car. KASPLAT! Guts gush out. The struck car sizzles. Smoke rises. And the ooze not only eats through the paint, but through the steel!

Keenan and his family clamber out of the lovebug-ruined car.

Baffled, Ash stares at the damage. "Did I do that?"

Keenan runs up to us, his family lagging behind.

"Aw, man," Keenan cries. "Talk about the worst birthday ever!"

A bundle of nerves, I shove my hands in my pockets. My knuckles bump against the orange Keenan's dad handed out earlier. I run my fingertips over the peel. For some reason the smooth, dimpled texture calms me. Just a little.

"We're heading to Harvey's Grove to take shelter," Keenan's dad says, approaching our group. "Kids, you're coming with us."

"Is there a way to get there and avoid the highway?" I ask.

Mr. Smith shakes his head.

"Lovebugs don't hurt humans, but they love black top roads and exhaust fumes," I say. "Since we can't avoid the road, we need to figure out how to keep them away from us."

Kelly starts to cry. Mrs. Smith uses her motherly magic to calm her, which makes me wonder if Lovebug and my mom are okay. I stare up at the mammoth flies flooding the sky. It's hard to believe that just an hour ago it was sunny and clear and I was snapping at my baby brother. Now it's overcast and gloomy and all I want to do is hug him.

I slip my hand into my pocket and touch the dimpled orange, hoping for another wave of comfort, when it hits. "Citrus!" I shout.

"Say, huh?" Ash's brows draw in.

"I know how to get us to Harvey's and home."

I quickly explain my plan, and with everyone on board, including Keenan's parents, we get to work. With the mega-bugs aiming for the highway, we're pretty safe over by the pavilion. Missy, Kelly, and I hunt for the ten super soakers and vests. Keenan, his parents, and Ash gather all the remaining oranges. They peel and juice the oranges into the water still sitting in the three refill buckets.

Once they've squeezed every last drop of juice out, we fill the water guns with the keep-away lovebug spray. For good measure, we rub our homemade concoction on all the vests, then suit up. Last, but not least, we spray all exposed skin with Bug Off insect repellent.

"Now remember," I say, "if any come near us, then blast them."

Ash leans into me and whispers, "Think this will keep us safe?"

Although I'm winging it, I give a confident nod.

Our super soakers at the ready, we march single file at a steady pace, the crunch of gravel under each step. Keenan's mom leads the pack, while his dad holds up the rear.

We move slow and deliberate. No one says a word. At the park, the super-sized flies drifted above our heads. Now by the highway, they also hover at eye level. This would've been so cool to inspect these insects up close, if it weren't a bug-apocalypse.

It's like a scene from that old Hitchcock movie, *The Birds*. Except instead of swift-zooming crows descending upon running people, there's wobbly-moving lovebugs plunging onto running cars. Traffic still creeps along with drivers struggling to see through bug-stained windshields. They swerve around abandoned vehicles, most dented, bent, or mangled. Smoke swirls from the damaged steel, whatever's left of the cars' hoods covered in dead mega-bugs.

Normal lovebugs don't make noise, but I swear there's this low buzzing, kind of like an electrical hum. It's deafening. Many continue moving north, heading toward I-95. It's as if their enlarged senses detect more traffic a few miles away.

"Keep your eyes forward," Mr. Smith calls out.

135

Of course, my gaze lingers on a drifting cluster among the wreckage. Many bulging eyes stare back at me. My breath quickens.

We're going to make it, I try to convince myself, thinking about my mom and brother. We have to.

The bugs jerk and lurch, bumping into each other. As a joined pair bounce in our direction, Ash repeatedly pumps his super soaker. He aims a ten-foot stream at the flies. The massive duo changes course.

Soon another lovebug couple bob and weave too close. Missy sends a fifteen-footer of citrus-smelling spray to chase the too-close-for-comfort buggers away. Not one lovebug is harmed.

I see the sign for Harvey's up ahead—no more than the length of a bowling lane—and start to believe we're in the clear. A sudden gust of wind sweeps a nearby flock in our direction. Kelly squeals. Mr. Smith jumps ahead of me, the cluster mere seconds above our heads, and grips a Honeybell in his raised hand.

I suck in my breath.

Pumping my soaker, I send a stream zooming at the flock, before Mr. Smith can launch at his mark. The keep-away spray knocks the bugs far away from us, completely unharmed.

I exhale.

"If you'd have killed them," I explain, "lovebug guts would've rained down upon us. If that can burn through steel, like it did your car, then…"

Mr. Smith's bewildered gaze slowly registers understanding. He wraps an arm around my shoulder and gives a tight squeeze.

We enter the grove's parking lot, occupied by a lone van, and run to the front door.

Mr. Smith bangs on the glass. "Harvey, it's me, Kel Smith!"

The second we're inside, Missy, Ash, and I huddle into a group hug.

"Hey," Missy pipes up. "I got a text from my mom. She's home safe!"

Once the sun has set and we've confirmed that the throngs of flies have cleared the road, we all pile into Harvey's van. First, we drop off Keenan and his family.

"Thanks for everything, Becky," Keenan's father says with a wide smile.

Next is Missy. She eagerly bounds up her driveway and leaps into her mother's arms.

Harvey pulls the van into my driveway. I jump out, waving good-bye.

"Don't let the lovebugs bite." Ash smirks.

I shake my head, "Too soon, Ash. Too soon," yet I can't help but grin.

The moment I reach the front door, I'm tackled by my baby brother. For once, his smothering doesn't bug me. I lock my arms around him and whisper, "Love you, Bug."

Zathwack! Pachow! Marmalade!

ZATHWACK! PACHOW! MARMALADE!

SEAN JONES

Nine-year-old Kylie in her ninja outfit could barely see over the steering wheel. She could feel the thrum of the anti-gravity plant and sense the power of the alien-bug technology in the hovercar. Lights from the gauges lit the vehicle's dark interior with a glow she found eerie. In the passenger seat, six-year-old Josh in his red swim-trunks squirmed and wriggled in his crash-harness.

"Careful of your burns," said Kylie. She felt guilty because she'd caused them. Too much kerosene when they'd torched the underbrush behind the farmhouse. At least, Josh wasn't injured critically like their little sister, Lynn.

"Can I shoot the machinegun?" asked Josh.

"You can't see in the moonlight," Kylie said. She wore infra-red goggles. "Wait until I turn on the floodlights."

Josh undid the buckles of his shoulder-straps and climbed up on his knees to look out the right-side window.

"Joshua Deane Watanabe," Kylie said. "Safety!"

"I want to look," he said, glancing around. "Why does Dad call this the Green Gobbler, anyway?"

"Green Goblin."

"That's not it."

Kylie let go of the broomstick she'd taped to the accelerator and the hovercar glided to a stop five feet above the short stalks of the soybean field ready for fall harvest. She took off her pink hat. *Lots of ninjas wear cowboy hats,* she thought. Flipping up her goggles, she let out a breath she hadn't realized she was holding and she rotated a dial on the dash that dropped the deflector-shields.

"Fine, Josh." *I can't let things fester,* she thought. "Headstrong Horse," Tiger-year Mom would call her. She handed Josh a pocket-notepad and a carpenter's pencil.

"And, do what?" he asked.

"Climb out while the shields are down and make a graphite-rubbing of him."

"Of the Gobbler?"

"Goblin."

Kylie knew Josh would need to be nimble at the pond if they were to save little Lynn. "Practice makes perfect," their mother used to say. *Dress rehearsal,* Kylie thought.

"Hold my feet." Josh wriggled through the open window frame. Ouch!" he said when his burned belly scraped the door-frame.

Kylie undid her harness, scooched over and held his injured ankles while he took the imprint of the emblem on the ancient vehicle's fender.

Don't turn the force-shield dial, she told herself. Dad had said anything in the plane of a shield coming active would be cut in half. He'd seen it when fighting in the Bug Wars, before humanity defeated the insect-like aliens, before people claimed and reused the anti-gravity and force-shield technologies in their cars and trucks.

Josh slid back in with the rubbing.

Kylie turned on the overhead red lights and looked at Josh's rubbing. "It says 'Gremlin.'"

"What's a gremlin?"

"It's not good." She knew a gremlin was something unexpected. Like burning your siblings.

"Can I shoot the rockets?" he asked. "At the bugs, when we get there?" He made squishing sounds with his mouth. "*Squeeshkkk, slurschk, smudddgggge.*"

Kylie dialed the shields up, flipped the infrared goggles down and pushed on the broomstick to make the hovercar go forward. "Josh, we can't use any ammunition." She glanced to see if he knew the meaning. He just pouted. "If we shoot anything that gets used up, Dad will know we took the Goblin, I mean Gremlin."

"Can I shoot the disruptor?"

Kylie smiled and looked at Josh, swerving only a little. "I was counting on it, Bro."

"Resilient Rooster," Mom had called Josh. "He doesn't stay down."

Soon, they arrived at the healing pond, its size a stone's throw across. "It's a vestige," Mom had said, a left-over site of alien technology, the waters known to hold amazing powers and, Kylie's goosebumps told her, something sinister.

She flipped up the goggles, put on her cowboy hat and brought up the Green Gremlin's floodlights. Dozens of giant bugs scuttled and scampered around the turquoise waters. They flew and flitted in the sudden brightness along the sandy shore. Millipedes like pythons, grasshoppers and crickets bigger than dogs, fire-beetles *and* smoke beetles with mandibles like blades, and at least two monstrous ticks, one of them with its jaws sunk into a pony-sized scorpion.

"Sick!" said Josh clapping his hands. He stood up and bonked his head on the reinforcement-bars of the roof. "Ow! I call disruptor. You said I could shoot the bugs."

"Let me get us over the water." She eased forward on the wooden broomstick and worried it might come untaped. A gremlin.

Bam! A tiger-moth the size of a Golden Retriever flew straight into the hovercar's front end, the insect's eyes frantic and searching, antennae groping, as it died.

"It knocked down the front shield," Kylie said. "I didn't know they had so much power."

"Regenerate, regenerate, regenerate," chanted Josh, half-closing his eyes, putting his hands on the cracked carbon fiber of the dashboard as if in blessing.

"Okay, full shields," said Kylie. "Your magic trick worked, Joshie." She wanted to encourage the little guy. Deflectors would come back in a second, in "one hurts" as Dad would say. *Why was it "one hurts?"* she thought. *Because you hurt the ones you love?*

The Green Gremlin hovered near the healing pond and Kylie tried to ease the hovercar forward but the broomstick came loose from the accelerator and they stalled. *In range of the ground bugs,* she thought. She powered up the disruptor.

"Start shooting, Josh. I'll fix the controls."

"On it." Josh scampered to the back and placed blistered hands on the weapon's grips.

Kylie scrunched down to fix her jury-rigged "gas pedal" and felt the hovercar shake and shimmy as giant bugs clanged into the shields.

"Zut-zut-zzzzuttt." went the turret-mounted disruptor, while Josh pivoted in the vehicle's rear compartment. He swiveled, swinging the alien-tech weapon in wild arcs.

"Sick!" he screamed and Kylie smiled, knowing boys loved guns.

But stealth and cunning are The Ninja Way, she thought.

"When you get a sec, hand me some duck tape, Josh?"

"Duct, not 'duck,'" he said. "I'm busy."

"Zzzutt, zut, zut," said the disruptor.

"Got one," Josh said. "Butterfly. Orange. Huge. Monarch. Dead."

"Go, Josh," said ninja-Kylie, rummaging for tape. She'd brought rope but had no way to cut it.

Blaaaammm, clang, thump! The Green Gremlin rocked from impacts.

"Josh, did you say, 'butterfly?'"

"Yeah. Yeehaw!"

"Don't kill those. When they explode, they damage the anti-gravity. How far was it?"

"A mile. Two miles."

Kylie shook her head. Must have been more than forty feet. She looked out the wire mesh where the vehicle's windshield would be and she remembered Dad's stories of how bugs from the road would commit suicide — the "S" word they weren't allowed to repeat — by flying into cars. *No windshields now and no cars,* she thought. *No Mom.*

"These are hard to hit," said Josh.

"You're doing great." Where's some duck tape?

"Hey, Ky, what's that big, black bug?"

The nine-year-old ninja-girl raised her head. "Cock-a-roach." She tried to do Mom's accent whenever she'd mention them from the old days. "Hit it with the disruptor. Those guys like to jump and ram."

"I missed! Look out."

Crunch! The Green Gremlin took a beating to the right side, knocking down the force shield and denting the armor, Kylie imagined. Dad could pull up a damage-display but she didn't know how.

"Regenerate, regenerate, regenerate," Josh chanted.

"Zzzzuuuutttt," said the disruptor.

"Hey, Josh, how did you turn on the TC?"

"What?"

"Targeting computer."

"The gunner works the disruptor. The pilot does the rest."

I don't know how to engage the TC.

She watched through the wire-mesh "windshield." There were so many bugs and Josh was missing them without the computer's help. He was making blasting sounds but he wasn't clearing a path to the healing pond.

"Can I have a try, Josh?"

"Nope. You called 'pilot.' I called 'gunner.'"

"Fine." *Fair is fair.* "I'm looking for—"

With a wallop, the Green Gremlin tilted to the right, "to starfish," Dad would say.

"What was that?" asked Kylie.

"What's orange with a bazillion legs?" Josh asked. "Here it comes again!" Josh made more shooting sounds while triggering the disruptor.

Kylie wished the weapon traced a beam but its blasts were invisible. The floodlights showed splashes in the healing pond's blue-green waters where the disruptor's blasts hit.

"Over land, we're a sitting duck," Kylie said. "Speaking of which, I still need tape—"

Crunch! The hovercar took a hit and Kylie felt it keel leftward, "to portabello" in Dad's words.

"How you doing, Josh? Hitting anything?"

"Kacheeng! Blowowowowow! Fazang!" he shouted. "Totally killing them."

"Bzzzt, zut, zit," said the disruptor.

A bald-faced hornet, extra-extra-large, pinged off the underside of the hovercar, banked around in the floodlights, and flew into the rear of the Green Gremlin, the monster's venom-tipped stinger stabbing, stabbing.

"Ky. Problem," said Josh, *"cachowing"* and *"bazinging."*

"Shoot it, Gunner Josh," she said. "Unless, you want to trade?"

A second hornet — or is it a wasp? Kylie wondered — joined the first and, then, a third. Yellow-and-black, striped, buzzing, thrumming, humming, the three of them probed with belly-spikes the size of harpoons. Every couple of "hurts," they'd hit and collapse the hovercar's rear shield. Then, the barbs would find a crack or crevice and penetrate into the cabin where Josh was.

"Bazazzaz!" said Josh. "Oh, sick. I hit the tick, Ky. The one that was riding the rack-nit."

"Arachnid? The giant scorpion? Is it dead?"

"It's attacking the other tick. This is so ill! *Braaaaappp, zizzzz, kathwappp.* The tick is hopping around on, like, seventeen legs. You gotta see this."

Kylie glanced up from rummaging in the tool box. "Josh, look out!"

A hornet's stinger found an opening and scraped across his bandaged back.

"This isn't working," she said. "It's too dangerous."

Ka-jamm! The Green Gremlin took another hit as an eagle-sized wasp thrashed the "starfish" side with its oversize stinger. *Ba-thunk!* Again.

Kylie climbed into the pilot's seat and cut power to the disruptor. *More energy for shields,* she thought. "Joshua, I need you up here."

"Tnineeeeni waaaaaaa shasham," he said, pivoting and swiveling the unpowered disruptor.

"Joshua Deane, now!" she said.

"Fine," said Josh. "I waxed most of them, anyhow." He backed into the front seat and Kylie could see in the rear-view that the three hornets were enlarging a hole in the back of the Green Gremlin.

"Ky!" said Josh. "Why didn't you tell me those bugs were spearing us? They could've gotten me. Why didn't you tell me to come up here?"

She shook her head. She knew they'd figure a way to pilot the hovercar home but she didn't expect they could cover up the night's outing. Too many gremlins. *Plus, we never lowered Josh down to the healing pond.* She didn't want to give up. *I can't let it fester.*

"Josh?"

"Ky."

"Did you know the gunner is sometimes the co-pilot?"

He frowned and, then, nodded. "Yeah, I know."

Clajang! A fire-beetle blasted a fireball and the shockwave washed over the hovercar.

"Come down below the seat and work the gas pedal. The skinny one."

Josh clambered over and pushed on the accelerator. The Green Gremlin rocketed forward, skimmed over the pond, going faster, faster, and Kylie could do nothing but feel them crash into a scraggly oak. *Varrrank!* went the hovercar as it creaked in protest.

"I knew you'd hit a tree," said Josh.

"Okay, Bro, let's try again. Let's—"

The Green Gremlin rocked as a smoke-beetle clambered onto the roof and discharged a soot-cloud, obscuring the floodlights.

"Reverse! Pull on the pedal gently and let go when I say," Kylie said.

"Pulling."

"Okay, not yet. Not yet. Okaaaayyyy."

The hovercar lingered over the pond and Kylie watched in fascination as the floodlights threw weird shadows of cavorting, giant bugs against the trees across the water. One of the oaks was clearly cracked, a gremlin-green stripe across its trunk.

"The ground bugs can't get at us. Come up, Josh."

Cruunnnsssssch! A blue dragonfly collided where the front met the side — the A-pillar, Kylie thought it was called — and she knew the damage would be obvious. She said, "Dad'll know we took the Green Goblin."

"Gremlin.

"Right, Josh. Anyway, flying bugs are too hard to hit with the disruptor. It'll be light before we kill them. If we kill them."

The dragonfly returned and collided with the rear hatch, where the giant hornets kept working with their stingers. The Green Gremlin lurched.

Kylie-ninja scratched her chin. "Do you trust me?"

"Sure, Ky. This is fun." His expression told her he was acting brave.

"You have to be bait, Josh."

"Bug bait?"

"Afraid so. Climb back to the disruptor."

"The hornets are doing something nasty."

"Trust me."

Josh looked at her a long time before he climbed into the rear.

Keep him distracted, she thought. "Make those noises again and rotate the disruptor."

"Zathwack, pachow, marmalade," he said, swiveling the unpowered weapon.

Kylie reached to the dash and turned down the dial for the shields.

In one, two, three "hurts," a hornet poked its curious and hideous head inside a hole the bugs had created. Kylie rotated the force-shield dial to full and decapitated the bug.

"Sick," said Josh but Kylie didn't think he meant it the way he usually did.

"Keep shooting, Bro. Confuse them."

She repeated the dial-decapitation. And, again. The inside of the Green Gremlin filled with beetle, moth and ladybug heads. Josh's favorite — the "sickest" — was the front half of a winged, white grasshopper.

When they'd exterminated all the flyers, Kylie ninja-tied their rope to Josh's crash-harness and he shimmied down into the healing pond, Dad's Army canteen in hand. As her brother filled and stoppered the green-plastic container, Kylie's "headstrong horse" instincts told her the turquoise waters would heal little Lynn's burns. "Trust your intuition," she imagined she heard Mom's voice whisper.

She said, "If you can be my co-pilot, Bro, I think we can make it home."

As he climbed up and entered the Gremlin, he asked, "Did I do it, Ky? Did I get the liquor?"

Flipping down her night-vision goggles and putting on her pink hat, the nine-year-old ninja smiled and told her "resilient-rooster" brother, "Not 'liquor.' Elixir."

"Will it save her?"

"Look, Josh." Kylie pointed to the pond, where the bugs they'd killed were twitching, growing back missing limbs and heads, healing.

"The pond works, Ky!"

She said, "I don't know what Dad'll do or what he'll say or how long we'll be grounded. It'll be bad. Very bad. But, trust me. When we've healed Lynn, he'll see it was worth it, Gunner Josh."

THE SECRET INGREDIENT

EILEEN NUNEZ

I warned my little brother Henry to stop asking Mom and Dad for those Science Kid Kits. I knew they were trouble. Well, now he believes me, after being held hostage by ants. It was Henry's genius idea to get the Shrink Kit. It claimed to shrink anything from a plastic straw to a leaf and then re-grow it with a special secret solution. Mom and Dad were happy Henry took such an interest in something educational. They said I played video games too much, but now look at where that got us.

Henry got too excited with the kit, poured too much of Bottle #2, and it exploded all over us in the backyard. The smell was like rotten eggs and tuna gone bad. We couldn't stop coughing; there was so much smoke everywhere. By the time the smoke cleared, and I got ready to noogie my little brother, I was surrounded by tall grass all around me. Like crazy tall as if I were in a cornfield! I turned and looked up. The science kit and the table were huge! I didn't know if everything around us grew, or to my fear, we had shrunk.

I got my answer when there was a tap on my shoulder, followed by a weird chirping sound. I turned around and my eyes bulged wide. Standing in front of me was a giant ant! It was at least three sizes bigger than me! I tried to run away but the guy had six legs! Four more than me if you're wondering, which makes him that much faster, plus he was so big. He

149

caught up to me and threw me over his back and carried me away like a tiny left over crumb.

I needed to find my little brother. If the same had happened to him, that meant he was even smaller! The ant zoomed through the grass faster than I could imagine. I was facing upward towards the sky. The ant was walking towards the now super giant apple tree that we had in the yard. I wanted to crawl off his back but it looked like I could break my legs if I jumped off of him. The distance to the ground was too far to land safely. I waited until the ant stopped near the tree. It grabbed me off of his back and threw me down towards a strange structure that looked like a pile of twigs.

"David!" I heard my little brother's voice. "Oh my goodness, you're tiny too!"

I wiped the back of my pants as I stood up. "What's going on Henry? Why are we in a twig prison? How is this even possible?" The ant had thrown me into a cell that was made of twigs and sticks. I tried with all of my might to push them aside. They couldn't weigh more than an ounce in reality, but for me it felt like it weighed tons.

Henry shied away looking guilty, his face reddening. "The ants, they are mad at us. Well, kind of more Mom and Dad, but they are taking it out on us."

"Henry, what in the world are you talking about?" I asked in frustration.

Henry took a pause to explain. "See, I shrunk first. I saw all the ants cheering when I was smaller than them. I heard them talking, and then they came charging at me, and brought me here. They also took the special ingredient bottle and carried it away."

I snorted, there was no way that he was telling the truth. "Henry, you're lying again, stop. You can't understand ants!"

Henry's eyes bulged bigger, the same look he gave mom when he wanted a donut before dinner. "David, I'm telling you the truth! They said that they want to keep us hostage, because mom and dad keep calling the exterminator! We're now their prisoners so that they can make Mom and Dad stop calling the exterminator and getting rid of germerations of their family!"

I looked at him, confused. "You mean generations?"

"Yeah! That!" Henry exclaimed.

"But how does us being their prisoner help them?" I asked.

Henry shrugged his shoulders. "I'm not really sure, but I heard that they are planning to attack the house."

I shook my head trying to figure a way out. "Okay, we need to get out of this prison, and find a way to make ourselves big again."

Henry looked at me. "We need the special liquid bottle, but the ants took it. We have to warn Mom and Dad."

I was feeling upset. "Do you know where they took it? Do you know what the special ingredient is?"

Henry shrugged his shoulders. "I don't know what the secret ingredient is. That's why it's called a secret." Henry then pointed towards the house. "I think they took the bottle to the ants' nest that was near the stairs of the house. They took it to their headquarters."

I rolled my eyes. "Henry! Now is not the time to play games! This is serious, we are literally smaller than ants!" I started to panic wondering how I would explain to my mom how I was smaller than a grain of rice. How could I tell my teacher that I couldn't do my homework because my pencil was too big for me? I walked in circles trying to think of a way out.

"Henry, do you have any ideas on how to get out of here, you were here first," I asked.

Henry looked around. "Not really, they just put me in here like they did to you."

"Okay, let's try to push the cage at the same time, maybe I can't do it alone, but with both of us, maybe we can move it or tip it over." We both walked over to one side of the cage. "On the count of three, we're going to run as fast as we can and push hard." Henry gave me an approving look.

"One...two...three!" We both ran fast into the twig cage.

"Ouch!" Henry yelled. "I think I have splinters now!"

That plan didn't work. The twigs didn't budge.

"Maybe we can dig our way out?" Henry suggested.

It wasn't the greatest plan, but it was all we had at the moment. We started to move some dirt with our bare hands. After some time, our fingers started to ache and all we had to show for it was dirty fingernails. I could just hear Mom saying, "Oh my, wash though filthy digits!"

We were running out of time. I knew dinner was getting close. I could see the kitchen light on. Mom would soon come out looking for us. We would be so small, she could crush us with her pinky toe! That would definitely ruin her day.

I sat in the dirt thinking of a way out while Henry kept running back and forth smacking his body into the twig cage. Something had to give. Henry continued running like a hamster smashing the twigs with no luck. I grew more and more annoyed, and hungry.

"Henry stop doing that!" I yelled. We started to argue back and forth and totally didn't notice the huge squirrel climbing up the tree. We kept yelling at each other until we noticed a dark shadow over us that slowly began to grow bigger. Henry and I stopped and looked up to see what the shadow was. To our horror, a normal sized nut was now barreling towards us looking like the giant meteor that took out the dinosaurs.

"Ah!" we both screamed. The nut smashed into the twig cage causing it to explode, throwing twigs and us all over the grass. I landed hard on my back and pieces of twigs fell over me.

Oh no. I had to find Henry and make sure he was okay. I rushed to my feet and called out to my little brother. I felt like I was in a cornfield and couldn't see anything but tall grass and the blue sky turning a gray color. *Here we go again.* If I didn't find Henry in time, we would be taken out by some rain drops and have to swim to the house!

"Henry!" I called out. I heard swishing in the grass. I stopped moving, but the grass kept swishing. "Henry?" No answer, but the swishing kept sounding.

Then, I saw what the swishing sound was. It was a group of ants rushing over to catch us! They saw the cage explode and didn't want us to get away. I started to run towards the house hoping to run into Henry, but I was also trying to stay away from the ants finding me. It was like being in the craziest maze with no way out. The only thing that I could follow was the sky and my now enormous house.

I could see the grass moving from side to side as ants in a line marched towards me, and another line marching in another direction. I moved between the grass blades to get farther away from the marching ants.

"David! Help!" I heard my little brother yell out. I looked over to my right where the other line of marching ants were, and they had found Henry and picked him up and put him on their back. They were taking him back to their headquarters!

I had to think quickly. I stopped and looked around me. If they had already taken Henry, the only thing that I could do now was run and try to get the secret liquid bottle and make us big again. It was too late for Henry, I was at least free and could try to escape the ants.

I decided to get down on my knees and crawl between the grass so I was lower to the ground and the ants wouldn't be able to see me. I crawled, and I was able to pass a few marching ants. I could even hear them talking.

"It's time to get that boy and bring him to headquarters to the Queen! She'll know what to do with them," said one ant.

The other ant sounded angry, "Yeah, we'll show them. We just have to keep that bottle as far away from them as we can. They'll never re-grow ever again!"

The two ants started laughing, and continued to march around looking for me. I stood as low as I could. I could hear Henry still yelling out for me to help him.

"David please! They are taking me to the Queen! I can't see the Queen! I'm scared!"

I didn't want to give up my position, but I also wanted to let him know that I was coming to save him. If only I had a better view. I looked around and saw the table. I could crawl over to the table where we were doing the science kit and then I could get a better view of where all the ants were!

It was the best I had so I quickly started to make my way over to it. It wasn't easy, and it was so far away from where I was. Normally it would take maybe four big steps from the tree area to where the table was, but now, it felt like it would take hours. I decided that I needed to run instead since the sky was now all grey. It was going to rain soon. I had no clue how the rain would be compared to my size, but I was pretty sure it wasn't going to be good.

One raindrop fell to my left and crashed into the ants. They all started screaming and telling the other ants to head back. "Head to the nest!" one ant ordered.

Panic started in my chest making it beat faster. If the ants were panicking, shouldn't I be if I was smaller than them?

I needed to hurry to find Henry and try to find a dry place. We could possibly get washed away if we weren't careful. I moved and dodged between raindrops. The rain started to get faster, and I still had no clue where Henry was. This was a disaster. I couldn't see where I was going so I just kept running. I heard something getting louder, almost like a missile, and it crash-landed on me.

That was it. I was a goner. The rain had gotten me and now it was coming full force. I closed my eyes and wished for it to be over fast. There was no way that we were going to make it out alive. The ants had won. I stood there lying on my back, knocked out from the raindrop and letting more take me out. It was a sad way to go.

"Boys! What on earth are you two doing? Get out of the rain! Wash up, dinner's ready," I heard my mom yell for the last time. She had no clue that we wouldn't be in for dinner, and it would be way too big for us to eat anyway.

"David?" I heard my little brother's voice sounding unsure.

I dared to open my eyes. I couldn't believe what I saw.

"Henry!" I exclaimed.

He was lying there right next to me, but he was back to his normal size! I quickly looked down at myself. I too had grown! It was a miracle!

"Henry! What happened?" I asked getting up from the ground.

Henry got up and ran over to where the secret ingredient bottle was, near the ant's nest. He picked it up and looked at it. On the bottle there was tiny print, small enough for an ant to read, that said, "Ingredient: Water."

"The secret ingredient was water!" we both yelled with relief and confusion.

I couldn't believe that we had gone through that crazy journey, and we accidently turned back to our normal selves. If it had never rained, we might have been stuck as human ants for the rest of our lives. What a nightmare!

Mom came back out and told us to come in already and get ready for dinner. "Oh dear, look at all of those ants! I guess we'll have to call the exterminator again." My eyes and Henry's widened, and together we both yelled, "No!"

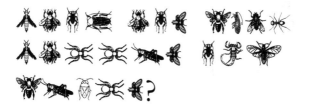

CURSE OF THE WERE-SPIDER

IAN C DOUGLAS

It does look like a skull," Mum said.

The car had just turned a bend. Dad was too busy driving to look up. Connor was hypnotized by his pad. That left me.

"Don't you think so, Brody?" she went on.

I nodded. Skull Crag had exactly the right name. A domed peak, eye-socket caves and tooth-shaped rocks. A shiver tickled my neck. Mum was ecstatic.

"The hiking will be superb!"

She returned to her guidebook. I pulled my collar up. Tramping up soggy hills might be Mum's idea for a fun weekend. It wasn't mine. Or Connor's. My big brother was sulking.

The car passed a sign draped in moss.

'Welcome to Grymm Tithing'

"So, we're there," Dad said.

The guesthouse emerged from the mist. It was a ramshackle building, with two pointy spires and a few missing slates. Huge pines surrounded it like furry green giants. The kind of place where a murderer might live. Or a monster.

Connor glanced up from his pad.

"Oh joy," he remarked sourly and returned to his computer game.

The swirling grey clouds exploded as we carried our cases to the porch. Rain thundered down on our heads. The landlady was waiting for us in the open door. She was tall and thin with full moon spectacles. Her hair was the color of pencil lead. She was smiling or maybe grimacing. It was hard to tell.

"You're late."

"Sorry about that," Dad replied. "The navigator got lost a few times."

Mum gave a 'hmph'.

"Yes, well, Grymm Tithing is a little remote," the old woman said, waving us inside. "You have to turn left at Pendlewitch. Everyone forgets that."

We were standing in a dark, wood-paneled lobby. A grandfather clock ticked slowly. The walls were decorated with paintings of old women.

"The Spindles have lived in Grymm Tithing for generations," the landlady said.

"Spindles?" Mum asked.

"My kith and kin," the landlady said. "I'm Veronica Spindle."

Dad held out his hand. Mrs. Spindle ignored it.

"You live here all by your lonesome?" Dad asked.

Mrs. Spindle sniffed.

"With my daughter, Lydia, yes. But you won't see her. She hides herself away. And I do not approve of her talking to boys."

She fixed Connor with a frosty glare. He swiped back his blond locks and rolled his eyes.

"A girl? Hardly."

"We'll live," I said, trying to cheer Connor up. He was sitting on the top bunk, looking glum. Our room was in one of the pointy spires. The windows rattled in their frames, mildew stained the walls and the beds reeked of mothballs. Our parents were in the bowels of the building, far away.

"No signal," Connor snapped and tossed his pad down to me.

"The Ferguson Boys have escaped worse fates than this."

Connor and I had faced some hair-raising situations in the past. Teamwork had saved our bacon time and again. But recently, well, Connor was changing. He'd grown two inches, for a start. His voice had dropped an octave. Blond fuzz was sprouting across his upper lip. Like that movie, *Invasion of the Body Snatchers*, Connor seemed to be turning into somebody else.

"It's Skull Crag."

I jumped in surprise. A girl was standing in the doorway.

"Blocks the Wi-Fi," she added.

This had to be Lydia, the landlady's daughter. Tall and gangly with ice-white skin. Her black hair was tied back, with a widow's peak.

I wrinkled my nose. Lydia smelled like a chemistry set. Connor was staring at her with his mouth gaping.

"You're gorgeous."

I couldn't believe my ears. Connor was going soft on a girl!

"Thank you," Lydia replied. The tiniest smile creased her lips.

"We don't get many guests my age," she added.

Connor slipped down from his bunk into an armchair.

"Um, so what do you do for fun around here?"

Lydia gave a slight cough to clear her throat.

"Not a lot. Well, I collect bugs."

"Bugs?"

"Spiders, flies, butterflies. I preserve them in glass boxes."

"Cool," Connor said.

Cool? More like creepy.

"Would you like to see?"

"Would I!" Connor cried and leapt to his feet.

He was acting really odd. Was he under some kind of spell? Could Lydia be a witch?

"Can I come?" I asked.

Connor and Lydia turned to me as they walked out of the room.

"I don't hang out with babies," Lydia said coldly. Connor snorted a laugh.

"Too right," he added.

They were gone. The bedroom suddenly seemed very empty. I chewed on my nails. There was something strange about Lydia. Something I couldn't put a finger on. Goosebumps were dancing on my backbone.

"All on your lonesome?"

It was Mum. "Here are your travel packs."

She placed them on the chest of drawers.

"Make sure you both bring them on the hike."

I prised the lid off one. There was an assortment of essential items, an energy bar, a torch, insect repellent, matches, a compass and antiseptic.

"Connor's gone off with that girl," I said.

"That's great, dear."

"Great! Supposing she's a—"

The words died on my lips. How could I say Lydia was a witch or a vampire? Mum would think me bonkers. Instead, I said, "they've left me alone."

Mum sat down beside me.

"Brody, Connor's growing up. He needs space."

"What for?"

She clucked.

"Now he's a teenager his interests are changing. You'll have to get used to it."

My throat ran dry. "Doesn't he like me anymore?"

"Of course, he does. Just give him time."

She gave me a big squeeze.

"You'll be the same one day."

Never! I thought.

A rickety old pool table stood in the basement; a room smothered in bottle-green wallpaper. The pool cue was cracked and likely to snap at any moment. I tapped the white ball, but missed the black by a mile.

"Where's the other one?"

I wheeled round in surprise. Mrs. Spindle loomed over me.

"I—I didn't hear you come in," I stammered.

"Quiet as a ghost when I need to be," she replied, frowning. There was a huge hairy mole on her forehead. The very sight of it made me feel like chucking up.

"Answer my question!" she demanded.

As much as Lydia gave me the heebie-jeebies, I didn't want to betray Connor.

"I think he went out for a walk."

Her eyes narrowed.

"With my daughter?"

"Um...no...by himself."

My cheeks flushed. I'm a terrible liar.

Mrs. Spindle peered up at the skylights. The pines were dripping rain.

"Seems unlikely."

She stared at me, as if she could read my thoughts. I looked for something to change the subject. A picture in a cobwebby old frame was hanging nearby.

"What's that?"

"Why are you asking?" she said. Now it was her turn to flush.

I studied the picture in more detail. It appeared to be a Victorian print. A spider as big as a horse was chasing a man across a moor.

Mrs. Spindle sighed.

"It's depicting the local folklore."

"Folklore?"

"The people of Grymm Tithing are a superstitious rabble. Delight in fairy tales and dark legends."

"About giant spiders?" I asked.

She nodded.

"A were-spider, to be precise."

"A what spider?" I said, shivering. A chill had settled on the room. She arched an eyebrow.

"Are all city boys slow-witted? You know what a werewolf is, don't you?"

"Of course."

"Then you should be able to figure out what a were-spider is."

She barged past me.

"Wait. Are you saying there are were-spiders around here?"

Mrs. Spindle paused in the doorway. Her eyes blazed with a strange emotion.

"I said legends. Fairy tales. Only a fool would believe such preposterous ideas."

She vanished into the gloom.

I fell back against the pool table, hands trembling. Instinct was telling me one thing. Sure, I was a lousy liar, but so was Mrs. Spindle.

The next day was no better. Curtains of grey rain swept down from Skull Crag. Mum and Dad gave up on their hiking plans. Instead, they opted for a trip into the village. This was my chance!

"My head," I groaned, rubbing my forehead.

"It's two aspirins and a morning in bed for you," Mum said.

They were both fooled by my fake headache. Only Connor flashed a suspicious glance as he dragged his reluctant heels off to the car.

Once they were gone, I explored the guesthouse. I tiptoed through the labyrinth of dark corridors, taking care not to be seen. Lydia's room was in the other spire. I knocked, but there was no answer. Pushing back the hefty oak door, I ventured inside.

Everything was old and decrepit. The walls were decorated with glass boxes. Each contained a dead butterfly, moth or beetle. Jars, bottles of chemicals and pins cluttered up her desk. The paraphernalia of preserving insects. The place had the same stink as Lydia. I guess that was the preserving fluid. Whatever it was, my eyes were stinging.

One glass box had a tarantula, as big as my hand. I stepped nearer. The body was like a soft, hairy tennis ball, while the legs were stripy. It was so well preserved it could have been asleep. My nose was almost touching the glass. And then it wriggled!

I lurched backwards so violently I tumbled over.

"What are you doing?"

It was Lydia.

I scrambled to my feet, heart pounding.

"It's alive!" I cried, pointing at the tarantula.

Lydia gave an icy smile.

"'Tis not. You imagined it."

163

She tapped the glass box. The spider remained as still as the dead thing it was.

I put my hands on my knees and breathed deeply. Maybe she was right?

"When's Connor getting back?" Lydia asked.

I stood up.

"You stay away from him."

She gave me a hurt look.

"Whatever for? He's my friend."

"You can't be friends with a were-spider."

There, I'd said it.

Lydia cackled. "You've been listening to my mad mother. No such thing as a were-spider. Obviously!"

"Isn't there?" I replied. "You keep away from Connor."

She edged closer. I could feel her breath of my cheeks, cold and rank, like rotting meat.

"Connor's a big boy. You don't tell him what to do."

"Wait till he finds out you're a were-spider. He'll dump you then."

Lydia put her hand on my shoulder. Her nails pinched my flesh.

"Then you better not say anything. After all, it's full moon tonight. All the spiders will be out hunting tasty flies. Flies like you. Now buzz off!"

I didn't need encouragement. I fled, with Lydia's laughter echoing in my ears.

"You can't go!" I cried.

Dinnertime had been and gone. Connor and I were in our room. Lydia had invited him for a moonlit stroll to see the caves on Skull Crag.

"I can do whatever I want, mate."

"Connor, no! Can't you see? Lydia's a were-spider!"

164

He roared with laughter.

"Why won't you believe me? I'm your brother."

Connor puffed out his chest. "My baby brother."

The words stung.

"I'm not a baby."

"You are if you believe in fairytales like that."

"Then why is your walk a secret."

Connor rolled his eyes.

"D'uh. Maybe so her loony mother doesn't find out."

It was no use arguing with him. Connor prided himself on being a rebel.

"I'm off," he said, swinging a leg over the open window. Fearless as ever, he grabbed a fir branch and disappeared into the night.

I sat on the bed, thoughts buzzing around my head like wasps. Connor had swallowed the bait, hook, line and sinker. Maybe Lydia had bewitched him. Who knew what powers a were-spider might have? Yes, she seemed truly fond of Connor, but didn't female spiders eat the males? It was no use going to Mum and Dad, they wouldn't understand. And Mrs. Spindle would hardly go against her daughter. No, there was only one person who could save my brother. Me. I clenched my fists and sprung to my feet.

The moon rolled out from behind the clouds, catching Skull Crag in a ghostly light. Two figures, hand in hand, disappeared into one of the eye-socket caves. I came out from the conifer wood and hesitated. Lydia was still human. Supposing I was wrong? After all, I didn't want an innocent girl to die.

"I'll have to wait till the last moment," I muttered. "Then go in for the kill."

My grip on the pool cue tightened. I'd broken off the tip and was using it as spear. I scrambled up to the cave.

"Isn't it romantic?"

It was Lydia's voice.

"Um, guess so."

Connor sounded as if he was having doubts.

I couldn't bear the tension any longer. With a ferocious yell, I stormed into the cave. And came to a complete stop.

They were sitting on a big stone. Connor had his arm around Lydia's shoulder. A couple of oil lanterns threw their flickering shadows across the rock face. Stars twinkled through a sinkhole in the roof.

"What the heck are you playing at?" Connor said, looking at me like I was bonkers.

The whole were-spider thing suddenly seemed a nonsense.

"Mum and Dad are so going to ground you," he went on, glaring.

"Can't I be alone with a boy, just once?" Lydia said in a sad voice.

I looked down. I'd really messed things up! But just then a moonbeam fell though the sinkhole. Lydia's ice-white skin began to gleam. A bout of coughing erupted from her lungs.

"Oh…I was hoping this wouldn't happen."

"What wouldn't?" Connor asked.

She walked a few steps away. The coughing fit grew worse and she collapsed onto all fours. She looked up, tears in her eyes.

"I'm sorry, Connor."

"For what?"

Lydia choked violently, as though something was trapped in her throat.

"I really…like you…you're cute," she rasped, trembling from top to toe.

"Aw, thanks," Connor replied, beaming.

"Connor!" I shouted.

"Enough with the spider crap," he shouted back. "Lydia's sick."

She was shaking and spluttering saliva.

"I didn't mean to eat you, Connor, honestly!"

"No worries, that's—what did you say?" His smile dried up.

Lydia let out a piercing scream as her face darkened. Her back swelled and heaved. All four limbs made a great tearing noise and split into halves. Now there were eight limbs. They grew longer, arched, and formed into segments. Green bile spurted from her lips. At the same time, her clothes ripped apart, as a bloated, bulbous body expanded out like a balloon.

The head was the worst. Her blackened skin crusted over. The forehead pushed down, burying her human eyes. Eight shiny black discs blinked into existence across the skull. Arachnid eyes! Her mouth, still screaming, widened. Appendages plopped out onto her chin. Two enormous mandibles, each tipped with a razor-sharp fang.

"Run!" I screamed.

Connor was paralyzed with shock.

A giant spider stood before us. Hairs were sprouting across its slimy back. The transformation was almost complete. We had moments to live! Brandishing the cue, I charged—too late. The spider reared up on its hind legs. It whacked me with one of its feet. I crashed against a boulder, banging my head. Red mist flooded my sight. The last thing I saw was Connor grappling with the monster. Fangs punctured his chest, sharp as a doctor's needle. Then I blanked out.

The cavern was cold and empty. A pain was throbbing behind my eyes.

"Connor!"

The horrifying events came back to me. My veins turned icy with dread, but I knew one thing. I had to save Connor!

The pool cue was nowhere to be seen. Picking up a lantern, I ventured to the back of the cave. A tunnel sloped down into the heart of Skull Crag. I followed its steep, twisting path, terrified Lydia might jump out at any moment.

Then the path opened up into a cavern. I lifted the lantern. Its glow revealed a hideous sight, the spider's nest! A jungle of thick, sticky webs, draped across a maze of limestone pillars. I was not alone. There were shapes dangling within the silky blankets, sheep, dogs, even a horse. But where was Connor?

I walked deeper into the cavern, taking great care to avoid the strands. The layers of web caught the lantern's light and reflected it back in a kaleidoscope of eerie patterns. Where was the spider? I turned a corner—and there she was! I saw her shadow on the webbing first. The way the limbs and jaws were moving sickened me. Then I gazed at the real thing. Lydia was spinning a boy-shaped bundle with her forelegs. Foamy liquid spewed from her mouth-parts and solidified on the bundle, like sugar turning into cotton candy.

"Put my brother down."

I no longer felt afraid. All that mattered was Connor.

Lydia obliged, delicately nestling his shrouded body within the nearest web. Eight eyes looked at me. She launched her attack!

Lydia hurtled towards me, fangs dripping venom. A screeching battle cry resonated from her thorax.

I'd come prepared, pulling a can from my jacket. The insect repellent from our travel packs. Just as her horrific face was upon me, I pressed the tab.

The jet of insecticide sprayed her eyes. She screeched furiously. We collided. I was knocked aside, while the blinded spider crashed into the web. I clambered to my feet. She was struggling against the gluey strands. I rushed up, spraying her mouth. Spider vomit gushed from her clicking jaws. Now to finish it. I tossed the lantern into the webbing. A fireball exploded.

Running over to Connor, I wiped the spider-spew from his face. A hard slap on the cheek woke him from the drugged sleep. I pointed to the inferno, and the spider within, shrieking as its blood sizzled and its limbs melted.

"We've got to go, Conn'."

Outside, we staggered down the hillside. Skull Crag belched smoke.

"We're safe," I said.

A bloodcurdling yell rang through the night. Mum! Connor and I exchanged horrified expressions.

"Mrs. Spindle!" Connor said. "The Spider's mother!"

"Must be…" but my words faltered.

Our parents were under attack. Spider attack!

"Come on" Connor cried, and we dashed into the darkness.

Marvin's Millipede

MARVIN'S MILLIPEDE

JANICE N RIDER

Marvin isn't a typical kid. I know because I'm his friend. My name's Lucy, and I've known Marvin since we were toddlers. I've always been attracted to people that stand out from the crowd, which is what Marvin does. Not that he looks unusual. He's an ordinary kid. If anything, he's homely. What's exceptional about Marvin is his passion for arthropods.

Hah! I can already hear some of you saying to yourselves, "Arthropods? What are those?" Well, I'm here to tell you. Arthropods are creatures that have multiple joints, segmented bodies, an open circulatory system (their blood is not enclosed in blood vessels), and an exoskeleton (they wear their skeletons on the outside instead of on the inside). Imagine if your skeleton was on the outside and your blood was sloshing around inside it! So, now you know why Marvin is different, really and truly different. I mean, how many people are crazy about arthropods?

Marvin's favorite t-shirt has the back end of a millipede on his back and the front end of a millipede on his front. It looks like the millipede has tunneled right through him. Millipedes are Marvin's favorite arthropod.

Millipedes have a pair of legs on most body segments. They have a lot of segments and an awful lot of legs, sometimes hundreds of them (but not thousands)! In our part of the world, most of them are pretty small, but you'll see them if you're paying attention when you're gardening. Marvin isn't much of a gardener, but when his dad is out gardening, he follows his dad around looking for the critters his dad unearths.

Last summer, Marvin and I found an American giant millipede in his dad's garden and decided to keep it for a while. It was over three inches long! Millipedes have few needs beyond a deep layer of moist soil and peat moss to bury in, some bark to hide under, and vegetables, fruit, and mulch to eat. In no time at all Marvin had his pet in a new home, a sizable aquarium. I wanted to call the millipede Lucille Liliana Lenox. When I suggested this name, Marvin scowled.

"Lucy," he chastised me, "can't you see that this millipede is a boy?"

I blushed. "It's a boy?" I repeated, wondering if, perhaps, Marvin was trying to fool me. He does do that sometimes. I looked at the creature's hind end in consternation.

Marvin rolled his eyes. "You need to pay closer attention to things. Male millipedes have modified legs, usually on the seventh segment from their heads."

"What?!"

"See, look here," he said, holding up the millipede and pointing. "Notice the gap where legs should be? There are modified legs tucked in there which hold sperm."

Awkward. I didn't want to know anymore. "Should have noticed that," I mumbled.

"You sure should have," he agreed.

Now, Marvin isn't my only friend. Sophia is also one of my buddies and, yes, she is also atypical. Her mom is a geneticist, and Sophia is as interested in genes (not jeans) as her mother. Growth hormones and gene response is Sophia's mom's specialty. It's kind of become Sophia's specialty, too, through a process of repeated exposure. If Marvin hadn't collected a millipede and Sophia hadn't been intrigued by genetic responses to hormones, we would have had a summer without mayhem and madness. Alas, it was not to be.

When Sophia eventually met our millipede, whom Marvin had dubbed Maverick Miles Maddox, MMM (you pronounce this as if you've just devoured something delicious) for short, she was fascinated. She loved the way his legs moved in waves on the sides of his body and the way he checked out where to go next with his antennae (due to his terrible eyesight). As she examined MMM through the thick lenses of her glasses, Sophia had an idea which, even at the time, seemed like a bad one to me. "Wouldn't it be marvelous," she commented, "if Maverick Miles Maddox was a substantial size?"

"No," I responded, "it would not."

"We could see everything better then. Right now, he's just so very little."

"He's an American *giant* millipede," I pointed out.

"Can't do anything about his size, anyway," Marvin shrugged. "But it would be cool if we could."

Sophia cocked her head to the side, a sign that the left hemisphere of her brain was in motion, and smiled. "Maybe, we can."

The next day the three of us, four of us if you count Maverick Miles Maddox, were together again. This time, though, Sophia had brought along a tiny tube with a hormonal cocktail in it. With Marvin overseeing the procedure, Sophia used a dropper to remove a couple of drops of the cocktail from the tube.

"Does your mom know what we're up to?" I questioned anxiously.

Pausing, Sophia caught me in a glance so ferocious I momentarily quailed. "No, she does not. Nor will she ever know. Got it?"

I nodded and shot a glance at Marvin. "Make like a scientist," he said and grinned. Yeah, I thought to myself, a mad scientist.

Marvin held out a piece of cucumber, a favorite of MMM's, and Sophia squeezed the bulb of the dropper. The viscous fluid was reluctant to drip, but eventually fell onto the cucumber piece. "Alright, Maverick Miles Maddox," Marvin said as he placed the cucumber in front of the millipede, "here is your lunch."

MMM began munching away. We all stared hard at the arthropod while he ate. He remained, to our eyes, precisely the same size. I sighed in relief.

For the rest of the day, Marvin, Sophia, and I discussed arthropods, genes, and ice cream (my intellectual contribution to our conversation). When we checked in on MMM before heading to our own homes and families for supper, he was burrowing into the soil. Only the last third of him was still visible. "Hmmm…" Marvin commented, with an emphasis on the "h." I was simply too hungry by then to pursue such a cryptic utterance. In retrospect, that "hmmm…" should have got me thinking, too, because, when millipedes shed their exoskeleton, they burrow under the soil to do so. It's easier to shed in the moist earth, and they're not visible to predators underground. You're probably wondering what the big deal is - well, millipedes shed in order to grow.

Upon my arrival with Sophia the next day, Marvin met us at his door with a broad grin and hazel eyes full of life, too full of life. "You've gotta see this!" he exclaimed and gestured for us to follow him to his bedroom where MMM was living.

Sophia gasped in disbelief and pleasure when she saw Maverick Miles Maddox. I gasped, too, in horror and consternation. The aquarium could no longer adequately contain our millipede. He was bent round on himself to fit within the tank's confines. I felt my stomach sink. "What are we going to do with him now?" I asked.

"We're going to take him out to my dad's garden! Isn't he awesome! He must be over a foot and a half long and has the girth of a skinny Dachshund."

I was selected to distract Marvin's mom during MMM's transfer to the garden. She's a high school physics teacher, so I made inquiries about how she was spending her summer. Delighted to have the opportunity for a conversation, she discussed books she was reading, a camping trip they were planning as a family, and the lack of interest the school board was showing in introducing the topic of quantum physics into the grade twelve curriculum. I pretended to be an attentive listener, but my mind kept sending out red alerts, which was entirely distracting. Finally, I made my escape to the garden.

Maverick Miles Maddox, now that the lid was off the aquarium, was flowing out of his habitat onto a cabbage plant. He made his way from there straight over to the cucumbers to begin some serious munching. My friends and I just stood watching MMM. It was the most incredible experience! It made me feel like I was part of something important. At that moment, none of us, not even me, were thinking ahead, not at all.

"Will your Dad be upset about his cucumbers?" I inquired.

Marvin was jarred out of the clouds by this question. "Oh. Yeah. He will be. But he never bothers with the garden until the weekend. MMM will be fine here for the next couple of days."

"What if Maverick decides to leave your parents' garden and wander somewhere else?"

"Maverick Miles Maddox, you mean," Marvin said. "And you do have a point, Lucy. Millipedes do most of their moving at night and ones much smaller than MMM have been known to travel fifty feet. So our friend could decide to migrate to someone else's garden. Considering his love of cucumbers, though, and all the mulch we have at the edge of the garden, I expect he'll stay here."

"We could put him in a bathtub," Sophia suggested.

"We'd have to fill it with dirt. Would your mom be alright with that?" I asked.

"We're going to leave him here," Marvin said. "He'll... "

Sophia gave Marvin a sharp look. "He'll be happier in the garden."

I opened my mouth to ask another question based on this strange exchange between my friends, then shut it again. Sometimes, it's best not to know things. One can know too much.

The next day was Thursday. All three of us were excited to see MMM. When we arrived at the garden early in the morning, though, we couldn't spot our arthropod friend anywhere. "Looks like he took a wander after all," I said.

The three of us hurried down the lane behind Marvin's house and garden. Four doors down from Marvin's was the Schultz place. Mrs. Schultz was a perfectionist, her lawn weed free and her garden bright with roses and peonies nestled amongst kale and lettuces. On this day, though, there was a hole that had been bored under some of her coral roses, causing them to tilt as if tired. I suddenly felt queasy. MMM was shedding again.

"I'm going back to my place to get some apples from the fridge," Marvin announced.

"Why?" Sophia asked.

"They're another favorite food. MMM can't stay in the neighborhood. We need to lure him up to the Hill. Apples are how we're going to do this. You two stay here in case he comes up."

Sophia and I turned towards one another, perhaps hoping to find comfort in a familiar face; however, Sophia had gone pale as paste (which wasn't comforting). I expect I looked equally anxious. Marvin ran back up the lane. Tentatively, we perched on the retaining wall beside Schultz's garden next to some flawless purple kale. We stared at the soil as if trying to dismember it with our eyes. MMM remained hidden. Marvin soon returned. He set the bag of apples he'd brought on the ground and surveyed the tilted roses with a somber expression. Then he spun around slowly, surveying up and down the lane, prior to picking his way over to the roses. Sophia and I watched, periodically checking the lane for people, as Marvin tamped on the soil beneath the roses and adjusted their positions so they stood at attention like showy soldiers. Next, he filled in the hole MMM had made. Clearly Marvin had learned a thing or two from his dad.

"When's Maverick Miles Maddox going to come out again?" I asked.

"Don't know," Marvin replied. "Sometimes millipedes burrow down to shed and stay down for days, but they can stay down longer. The other day, MMM molted fast. Could be the result of the hormone cocktail Sophia gave him. Also, he may have burrowed underground to avoid the light of day. Millipedes aren't keen on sunlight."

"Well, you two might want to stay here for ages waiting for your arthropod to come up, but I'm not willing to fritter away my time like this!" Sophia snapped.

"Don't forget whose idea it was to use growth hormone on him!" Marvin retorted.

Sophia slumped as she sat. "If Mom finds out what I've done, she's going to kill me."

Maverick Miles Maddox did not come up on Thursday. On Friday morning when we checked out Schultz's place, there was no sign of him having come up either. By Saturday, Sophia said she had lost interest in keeping tabs on MMM. I think that it wasn't interest she lacked, but nerve. She was probably wondering just how big MMM was going to be when he showed himself next. I was anxious about this, too, but my curiosity drew me to Mrs. Schultz's garden time and again. On Sunday evening, about nine o'clock, Marvin and I slipped down the lane, Marvin with his bagged apples on hand as usual. Since millipedes don't like being out in the sun, we figured he was most likely to dig his way to the surface in the evening, at night, or in the early hours of the morning. Our visit was rewarded. Not long after our arrival, we watched in dread as the middle of the garden heaved, displacing lettuces and carmine peonies. An enormous head reared above the earth. Segment after segment followed MMM's head, each with these huge legs attached. The garden pitched and rolled as vegetables and flowers tumbled into complete disarray. Our millipede must have been as long as two grown men placed end to end. I glanced at Marvin. His lower jaw was dropped, his eyes bulged, and his legs trembled. And then, to my astonishment, he whispered to MMM, "You are magnificent!"

My friend had come unhinged. It was the only explanation for those words. I needed to bring Marvin back to Earth. "We have to get him to the Hill. Everyone will want to destroy MMM. They'll be afraid of him. I'm afraid of him! Pull out an apple."

The Hill is an inner-city park that's been set aside as a natural area. This seemed like a suitable place to lure our friend. The apples Marvin had on hand were now slightly soft, working towards a decomposed state. As the first apple left the bag, Maverick Miles Maddox wiggled his antennae. Antennae in millipedes are available for tasting and smelling at one and the same time. Clearly, MMM was aware that an apple was nearby in spite of his terrible eyesight. He came our way. Marvin and I took off at a gallop down the lane, Marvin waving the apple frantically in order to leave a chemical signature in the air. MMM followed behind us, large legs rising and falling rhythmically. My heart was pounding away faster than my feet. Just as MMM was about to catch up to us, my friend dashed his apple onto the ground. I actually heard our arthropod crunch into it. If I'd been running fast before, I was almost flying now. The Hill was blocks away from where we were. How would we keep up this pace?

As we reached the end of the lane, both of us turned right. Marvin was now waving another apple over his head. I peeked over my shoulder and saw that MMM had resumed the chase. Soon, we would be passing Sophia's house. Ahead of us, a neighbor, Paul Teague, was strolling in our direction with his golden lab, Lucas, at his side.

"Run!" I screamed.

Paul appeared confused and Lucas launched himself at me in a boisterous hello that knocked me flat. MMM emerged from the lane at this moment, prompting Paul to let out a yell that would have scared spots off a jaguar. Lucas was momentarily immobilized by the sight of the monster hastening his way, but soon recovered enough to yelp, tuck his tail in between his legs, and bolt off in the opposite direction. Paul was spun about on his heels only to crash to the ground. He was dragged off in the wake of his lab.

Meanwhile, I finally had my feet back under me and was in pursuit of Marvin who was a full nine yards in front. As I flew past Sophia's house, I saw that she was framed in the window, her eyebrows riding high over her eyes. No doubt they rode even higher when Maverick Miles Maddox came by.

My heart leapt with eager anticipation when I spotted the Hill. Marvin turned towards me at its base, stopping. MMM was so close behind that I felt an antenna graze the top of my head. An apple sailed over me and I snuck a look at the millipede as he reared up to catch the apple in his mandibles, rather like a dog might catch a stick. Juice from the fruit rained down on my head. My friend had given me the time I needed to keep ahead of our arthropod. Soon, Marvin had my hand in his as we ascended the flank of the Hill with gasps and groans, weaving amongst poplar trees in the hope of slowing Maverick Miles Maddox's pursuit.

Cresting the Hill, my legs gave out. "Get up, Lucy!" shouted Marvin, grabbing my arm and pulling me back to my feet.

MMM was lacing his way through the trees like some enormous beige thread, eager as a hound tracking a hare. Marvin rolled some apples in his direction, then deposited the rest on top of the Hill. It worked. We disappeared into the darkness as Maverick Miles Maddox feasted on Honey Crisps and Jonagolds.

My parents were furious when I arrived home after ten o'clock. I had barked my knees and bruised my shins. Mud and leaves were clinging to my shirt and shorts. My explanation was that Marvin and I had been climbing trees (something we still liked to do) and running races. My dad who has a stubborn, competitive streak (a consequence of being a phys ed teacher) asked if I'd won most of the races. "The most important one," I said.

"Good for you. But now you must go straight to your room and bed, young lady," he commanded.

"But have a bath first," Mom added.

Baths and bed are usually low on the list of things I want to do, but on this night I was grateful to do as my parents bid me. I couldn't remember ever feeling so utterly weary. The instant my head hit my pillow, I was asleep.

In the morning, when I entered the kitchen, Paul Teague was there with his yellow lab. Poor Lucas was hiding beneath the man's chair, shaking like the proverbial leaf. "Tell your parents what happened last night," he demanded.

"Ummm…" I started, and then there was a knock on the door.

Mom opened it. On the porch stood Marvin, with dark circles under his eyes, and Sophia, with a bright smile plastered on her face. The sight of our neighbor gave Marvin a start, and the circles under his eyes became even darker.

"Hello, Mr. Teague," Sophia said chattily. "It's wonderful to see you. I saw you out with Lucas last night."

"Then you can corroborate the sighting of the beast that precipitated itself out of the alley towards Lucas and me." Paul Teague invariably spoke in this fashion.

"Sighting of a beast?" Sophia pretended to be befuddled. "I only saw you and your dog. I saw him haul you away after he knocked my friend over, if that's what you mean."

When Marvin and I also refused to verify spotting a huge predatory "worm," Paul Teague became miffed. At this point, Marvin approached him. "Is this what you saw?" he inquired, opening up a fist to reveal an American giant millipede, one the size all such creatures should be. Paul Teague frowned and bit his lip.

"Alright. We'll confess, or I will. The truth is," said Sophia, "we were playing with the creation of a hologram of this tiny millipede. Sorry. We didn't mean to frighten you as badly as we did."

Paul Teague left my home in a huff, leaving my friends and I to be chastised by my parents. It felt like we deserved to be berated and, as a result, we took our scolding without complaint. Following our tongue lashing, I grabbed a bowl of cereal and headed outside with my friends.

"That isn't MMM," I said to Marvin, nodding at his gently closed fist.

"No, it's not," he responded, carefully placing the arthropod in some mulch at the side of the house.

"Where is MMM, then?"

"He's... he's disappeared down into the ground again. Looks like he could be on his way to a city north of us."

So the next time the earth trembles and shakes, it could be Maverick Miles Maddox. Please. Do us a favor. Feed him some apples or cucumbers and tell him we're sorry for disrupting his life.

BUTTERFLIES

PETE WOOD

Ruth parked her beat-up hatchback about fifty yards from Mom's farmhouse. A giant butterfly, larger than her car, sprawled across the dirt driveway.

Casey, her brother walked up. "Think we can handle the bug?"

"It's not even that long." She was not in a good mood. Her second tenure panel in five years had bombed. Nothing had pleased Professor Steiner, the Biology Department Chair at NC State University.

The butterfly's wingspan was greater than a school bus. The creature munched on crabgrass and waist-high pokeweed. Its stench, like rotting garbage, made her stomach lurch.

Casey laughed. "I'll get us some help, Professor."

"I'm still not a professor."

"That sucks. Sorry, Sis."

He whistled and his border collie, Scooter, ran up and sat at his feet. Casey could train anything.

Ruth wondered if Casey had even left the house he still shared with Mom today. He said Mom needed the company after their Dad passed away. Sometimes he had landscaping jobs. "Where's Mom?"

"In the house. She couldn't stand the smell."

The front door creaked open. Wearing a long paisley housecoat, Mom stepped outside. "Are you two going to do something about the bug?"

183

"Yes, mom," Casey called out. He looked down at Scooter. "Tree."

Scooter raced away and stopped under an enormous oak and waited for Casey's next command.

Mom turned to Ruth. "I missed the Church Social today. I couldn't get out of the driveway."

Ruth just wanted to have a good stiff drink and forget her day back in her own apartment. "Mom, we can't just haul the butterfly away. It has to be studied."

Casey ran his fingers through his long hair. "You didn't tell NC State, did you, Professor?"

"I told you, I'm not a professor." Ruth sat down on the steps to the front porch. She hadn't realized how tired she was. "I had to. I work there."

"I wish you hadn't. We could have dragged it across the property line onto University property. Make them figure out what to do, instead of having them camp out on Mom's property for days."

The gate to NC State's teaching forest was only a football field's length away. Her deceased father, a biology professor at NC State, had picked the house years ago because the forest was so close. It was just like Casey to dump his problem on somebody else.

Still, Casey made sense. The University would be getting involved anyway. "I didn't think about that."

A car horn blared. A jeep pulled to a stop behind Ruth's car.

The University's Entomology Field Team had arrived.

Professor Steiner jumped out of the jeep. He wore khaki pants and a bulging multi-pocketed vest like he was on safari. He grabbed a knapsack and motioned for his posse of grad students to follow him.

Ruth stared at Steiner. Why did they send the department chair to handle a routine entomology issue? Large insects were hardly unique. NC State catalogued fifty or sixty a year, just in central North Carolina alone.

What really gnawed at her was that nobody had contacted her and asked for her input. Somebody in the Department could have asked the biology instructor who had phoned in the report to join the team.

The butterfly cocked its head and glanced at the jeep. It returned to grazing.

A bearded student in a tie-dyed t-shirt pulled a tranquilizer gun off the backseat and handed it to Steiner. The professor aimed it at the butterfly.

Steiner squeezed the trigger and a dart hit the butterfly. The creature let out a low-pitched moan and slumped to the ground.

Steiner barked orders at the grad students. They pounded knee-high metal stakes into the ground around the unconscious insect and connected the markers with billowing red tape. It looked like a crime scene.

The students unfurled a large net over the butterfly. They snapped steel cables into place, grounding the net.

Ruth walked over to Steiner and forced a smile. "Good to see you again, Professor."

Steiner wore mirrored sunglasses and flashed a perfect salesman's grin. "It was a shame your father couldn't have been at that meeting today. He would have put in a good word for you."

All Ruth could manage was an anemic "Yes, sir."

Steiner pointed to the grad students. "I need to attend to my field workers."

Casey jogged up. "Afternoon. I'm Casey, Ruth's brother. That butterfly wasn't going to eat us, was it?"

"Your Dad had some nice gatherings out here back in the day." Steiner shook Casey's hand. "I guess your sister never told you that butterflies are vegetarians."

"Nope," Casey said.

Steiner winked at Ruth. "Did you miss that class, Ruth?"

"I've taught an upper level entomology class for five years," Ruth said.

Steiner nodded. "Oh, that's right."

A breathless grad student with long dreadlocks ran up. "Sir, the insect's secure. We're ready to take tissue samples."

"I'll collect the samples," Steiner said.

The student blinked. "Um, sure, Professor Steiner."

Ruth had been part of many an entomology team. Taking DNA samples to determine the stability of the creature's genetic makeup was grunt work, not something for department chairs.

Steiner set his knapsack down and removed a small toolbox. He gently applied a scraping tool to several exposed areas of the insect. He placed the tissue samples into baggies. "It's a latent mutation."

"What are y'all talking about?" Casey asked.

"If the bug—" Ruth began.

"Butterfly," Steiner corrected. "Hespeniidae magnissima."

Ruth knew her bugs, but had never heard that Latin phrase before. Steiner had undoubtedly just made it up to impress the grad students.

"Butterfly," Ruth continued. "The DNA spectrum analysis will determine if this is a latent mutation or a recent mutation like the ants that overran Los Alamos back in '91. A recent mutation would mean that somebody's breaking the law and messing around with radiation and DNA. A latent mutation would be a side effect from the atomic testing in the fifties and sixties."

"Correct." Steiner put the tissue kit back in the knapsack. "My students are going to set up a couple of traps in case some more butterflies appear. We'll remove the trapped bug when our truck gets here."

"You expect more butterflies?" Ruth asked.

Steiner reached into his vest and pulled out a bottle of water and took a sip. "Seasoned biologists have a feel for these things. You'll understand someday, Ruth."

Mom stood at the door to Ruth's old room. She wanted both of her children to stay as long as there might be monster bugs in the yard. "Can I get you anything, dear? Another blanket?"

Ruth just wanted to lie down for a few minutes after dinner. "I'm fine, Mom."

"I don't understand why you can't find a nice man and settle down."

Ruth wasn't sure what was more annoying — her Mom's constant meddling in her dating life or the fact that Mom just didn't want to understand who she was. "Mom, you know I date girls."

"What about that nice boy who took you to prom?"

"Good Lord, Mom. That was almost twenty years ago. Stan Hubbard's been out of the closet for a long time."

Casey called out from the living room and rescued her. "Give it a rest, Mom. Ruth's doing just fine."

Mom showed a sad little smile. "I just want you to be happy, dear." She closed the door.

Ruth studied her childhood bookshelf. The problems of Nancy Drew seemed overwhelming before Ruth had to contend with a terminally ill Dad and an alcoholic girlfriend. Of course, Nancy Drew had a father and friends who supported her career. Even the police took a teenager seriously as a crime solver.

A loud buzzing, like a chain saw, interrupted her musing. Something crashed against the house. Scooter howled from the yard.

Somebody knocked. Ruth prayed it wasn't Mom with more dating advice. "Come in."

Casey walked to the window. "There's another one of those bugs."

Ruth yawned. "Butterfly?"

"It's a dragonfly."

Ruth peered outside. The monster dragonfly, bigger than a S.U.V., hovered an arm's length away. Its jaws snapped at the air.

Scooter sat under the oak tree and barked.

"That thing eats plants, right?" Casey asked, pointing to the large jagged mandibles.

Ruth shook her head. "They're carnivores. The little ones eat mosquitos and gnats and flies. I don't know what the big ones eat."

.

Ruth and Casey had no trouble convincing Mom to stay in the house. They stepped outside. Casey held Dad's old shotgun.

With a thunderous buzz, the dragonfly slammed into the front porch. Its wings jammed against the posts. It couldn't get any closer.

Casey fired the shotgun.

"Don't hurt it," Ruth said.

"Just trying to scare the sucker."

Startled by the noise, the creature flew off and focused on Scooter. In a strafing maneuver, the dragonfly dove down to the dog. Scooter darted behind the tree. The dragonfly couldn't force its oversized wings through the tree's sprawling limbs.

"You got enough ammo to keep scaring it away?" Ruth asked.

Casey popped another shell into the gun. "Sure."

Ruth pointed to a net Steiner had set up by the oak tree. "I'm going to get the bug into the net."

Casey's eyes opened wide. "You sure you know what you're doing?

"I'm a biologist. Let's go."

The dragonfly was preoccupied with Scooter. Ruth made it to the edge of the net in a couple of minutes. Casey stayed a dozen paces behind.

Ruth knew she should be terrified, but she just felt exhilaration. After unclear goals the last few years, outwitting a ravenous insect was straightforward.

"What now?" Casey asked.

Ruth pointed to the trap's switch. "One of us needs to pull the switch when that thing lands. I'll get that bug's attention."

She started screaming.

The dragonfly ignored her.

Ruth yelled louder. "Hey, stupid! Over here!"

"Maybe the bastard can't hear you," Casey said.

How had she forgotten something from High School Biology? Casey was right. Dragonflies felt vibrations in the air. The shotgun burst had created enough of a ripple to startle the insect, but dragonflies didn't hear.

"Fire some shot close to it," Ruth said.

"I have a better idea." Casey whistled and Scooter looked at him. "It's a little hunting trick. I call it serpentine."

Scooter stared expectantly

"Get the duck!" Casey yelled. He threw a stick to the far side of the net and let out three quick whistles.

Scooter ran a crisscross pattern in front of the dragonfly.

Casey kept the shotgun aimed at the dragonfly as it dove towards Scooter.

It skimmed across the steel mesh and Ruth flipped the switch. The trap clamped shut. The dragonfly thrashed and bit at the cables. The net held firm.

Scooter rested at Casey's feet.

Casey scratched the dog's head. "Good boy." He turned to Ruth. "Sis, where'd that bug come from? Is it another latent mutation?"

"Nope. And neither is that butterfly."

"That professor said—"

"Steiner's lying." She looked towards the teaching forest. Broken sapling and torn shrubbery showed where something had punched its way out. "We need to check out the woods."

Casey pointed to the sun which was dipping below the horizon. "If it's all the same to you, Sis, I'd rather wait until daylight."

The next morning, Ruth and Casey entered the forest.

Ruth stopped at one of the signs that described some unique forest feature. "Dad played this game with the signs. He wanted me to memorize them from our last hike. He used to tell me what a good biologist I'd be. Did he ever tell you that?" Ruth said.

Casey laughed. "The only game Mom and Dad ever played with me was pretending that I'd go to grad school like my older sister."

"Mom's favorite game is pretending that my girlfriend is a really good friend."

Casey sighed. "Yeah, she lives in her own world, doesn't she?" He kept a firm grip on the shotgun. "What are we looking for?"

"I'll know when I see it."

"What's that over there?" Casey asked.

A nondescript gray building nestled in low-lying branches and vines. A faded sign said MAINTENANCE.

A colorful red umbrella, like one beside a beach motel's pool, poked over the roof. They walked closer and Ruth realized it was a mutated flower, as tall as a tree.

Casey let out a low whistle. "Holy crap."

He jimmied the shed lock with his pocket knife while Ruth held the shotgun. Inside, grimy fertilizer bags and rusty tools sprawled on rotten shelves. The shed looked like it hadn't been touched in years except for shiny new lockers near another door.

Ruth opened the lockers. A heavy black gown hung inside. A stack of gloves and hoods rested on the top shelf atop a closed laptop.

"The clothes are lead. Somebody's monkeying around with radiation." Ruth rapped on the interior door. "Whatever we're looking for's in there."

"Allow me." Casey grabbed a flathead screwdriver off a work bench and fiddled with the deadbolt. After a couple of minutes, he pulled the door open.

Ruth handed a gown to her brother. "Put this on."

It was hard moving around in the lead clothing and the hood's glass plate kept fogging up, but Ruth still recognized a lab when she saw one. She noticed metal counters, covered with neatly stacked folders.

The base of one wall was rotten. She could see daylight through a hole that was partially patched with duct tape. This lab hardly met the industry standard for a "clean room".

Against a wall were large glass domes. Peeking inside one, she saw what looked like a good-sized trout swimming in a foot of water.

It was a tadpole.

Ruth imagined somebody rummaging through the Biology Department's dumpster and cannibalizing discarded lab equipment. Rubber tubing connected x-ray tubes, old-style incubators and centrifuges. Bottles of colored liquid — probably mutagens— filled one shelf. A very expensive electron microscope stood out among the scavenged parts.

Then Ruth saw the Woolworth's Home Reactor. She had read about the now-defunct retail chain that had tried marketing atomic power in the seventies until Three Mile Island bankrupted them. "Those things are illegal."

Ruth slammed the lab door. She hurled her gloves onto the floor and let loose a stream of profanity.

Casey crossed his arms. "What the hell, sis?"

"That s.o.b. acts so high and mighty and he's breaking the law."

"Steiner?"

"Yeah." She didn't know what made her angrier — that Steiner wasn't playing by the rules, or that he was literally conducting experiments in Ruth's backyard and hadn't included her. If he had asked for her help, she wondered if she would have agreed.

"So, do something about it."

Ruth slowed down her breathing. She glared at Casey. "Like what? He's Department Head."

Casey shrugged. "Something besides complaining."

"The bastard turned me down for tenure."

Casey rolled his eyes. "Yeah, I know."

And, without thinking it through, Ruth pulled out her mobile phone and called Steiner.

Steiner arrived in half an hour. He wore jeans and a sweatshirt. His hair stuck straight up, like he had just awakened. He frowned at Ruth. "What are you doing here?"

Ruth stayed calm. "Professor Steiner, why do you have an atomic reactor?"

Steiner shrugged. "The ban on genetic radiation experimentation is pointless. Mutations aren't necessarily bad if they can be controlled. Evolution is mutation." He leaned against the wooden shelves. "Why'd you call me down here? Are you trying to strong-arm me into doing something? Do you want tenure that bad?"

"You should have given me tenure yesterday."

Steiner sighed. "Why? Because your Dad used to run things?"

"I've earned it. Last time you told me I needed to write more journal articles. I've had eight published in three years and I still haven't done enough?"

"Ruth, lots of people get denied tenure. Some people never make it."

"Yeah, well maybe the guy running things shouldn't be breaking the law. Maybe I should call the cops right now."

"Ruth, that's not going to help things." He closed his eyes for a second. "Maybe you do have to prove yourself more, because of your Dad. Maybe some folks resent you."

Casey put his hand on his sister's shoulder. "Sis, you need to calm down. He's got a point. Daddy did get you your first job down at State."

"That was a long time ago," Ruth said.

Casey turned to Steiner. "And, it wouldn't hurt if you got along with folks better. You sure didn't make any friends yesterday around this place. You didn't even talk to my Mom before you started tearing things up."

"You're right. I was pretty rude," Steiner said. "But you two are looking at my DNA project all wrong. I've filled out the forms with the EPA. This project will be approved."

Ruth laughed. "That almost never happens"

Steiner glared at her. "I think I can walk my way through a government form."

"Nobel laureates can't get approval half the time."

Steiner snorted. "I suppose you could do better?"

"Maybe I could." Ruth sketched an idea she was contemplating for her next journal article. She handed the sketch to Steiner.

Steiner glanced at the diagram. "What is this?"

"It's a dual virus approach for genetic manipulation. One virus mutates an isolated strand of DNA. The other virus protects the remaining strands from radiation. With better radiation shielding and these two viruses, I think the EPA might give you a waiver."

Steiner smirked and studied her drawing. His smirk vanished. After a minute he said, "And this one on the left, the alpha virus, I'll call it—"

"Attacks a specific strand of DNA."

"And the Beta virus?"

"Protects the remaining strands. No more surprises."

Steiner sat down on a chair. "Ingenious."

Ruth squeezed Angela's hand. This was her first trip to Mom's with her new girlfriend. She and Angela had dated for three months after meeting at the southern university symposium in Greensboro. "Honey, you need to understand a couple of things. My mother's place is a little unusual."

Angela drummed her fingers to the reggae music on the radio. "I have a mother too."

Ruth pointed at the woods. "The project's in there. Steiner and I have to get the place shipshape for another EPA inspection on Monday."

Angela frowned. "I guess that means you'll be home late."

"Yeah, but on the bright side, Steiner says things are looking real good for tenure at the next review." She turned down the driveway. "Mom has a bit of a butterfly problem."

Angela looked puzzled. "So?"

Ruth parked the car. "Take a look."

Casey stood beside a recently felled loblolly pine. A monster butterfly hovered nearby. Casey flashed a flashlight at the bug and it landed beside the tree.

"He's trained the bugs," Ruth said.

Casey looped a rope around the butterfly. The creature turned its head as if expecting something. Casey fed it a long piece of pokeweed. When the bug finished its treat, Casey aimed the flashlight at the butterfly's eyes and clicked it off and on several times. He whistled twice and Scooter barked and ran circles around the bug.

The butterfly rose into the air, like a helicopter. Scooter ran off to a far corner of the yard. Carrying the tree, the butterfly followed.

"His landscaping business has really picked up," Ruth said. "He has four butterflies and a dragonfly working for him.

"Sweet lord," Angela gasped.

Ruth turned off the engine. "But listen, it's really going to get weirder."

"How could it possibly get stranger?" Angela asked.

Ruth stroked Angela's long blond hair. "If Mom gets you alone, she'll ask if you have a brother I can date."

Sisters of the Long Year

SISTERS OF THE LONG YEAR

MICHAEL A. CLARK

I hadn't eaten in over three years. So, hungry, I strode out into the open.

The web was quiet at first, the random vibrations telling of snap breezes and shifting clouds, the flap of an owl's wings. All the girls had repairs to do before they could talk.

The year was still damp and new when the first stirrings in the strands came. Betty had snagged a fly at first light and was just wrapping up her first serving. She dwelled in a poor location, deep amongst some maple limbs. She was too far back from the open trail to easily reap the commute of beetles and moths. I felt happy for her, through the eternal doubt of when my next meal would come.

"You go, girl!" I said. It would take time for her to respond, and I had to attend to other matters. A leaf was stuck halfway across my web. Hanging in midair, it signaled stay away to potential prey. The leaf was waving back in forth in the stiff breeze. I had to cut it loose, hoping it wouldn't drag the web (and me) down with it. Down to the Ground, where danger ruled.

I hate the Ground.

"Thelma lost half her web," Betty said. "To a blundering raven during the Dark. She lost the rest of the meal she'd caught last year, too."

Things are tough all over, I thought. A year at least for Thelma to re-weave, and on an empty stomach.

I thanked the Great Spinner, Weaver of the Dim Lights above the Dark, that such misfortune hadn't struck me. A leaf here, a torrent of rain there, but I'd been fortunate over the past 75 years or so. My strands held firm and I ate regularly, if not always well. Then there was the one time, when I fell to the Ground...

But I needed to focus on fixing my web. I went out on the central strand and paused, scanning for danger. The breeze was cooler, as it had been for the past several years. No shadows of death darted above. Nor the tread of a sister on my strands.

We love each other, we sisters of the long year, and talk on the slender strings of our slim webs. But we never meet, as sisters are just prey to each other. Like the hapless males upon whom we feast.

Seems cruel in a way. But that is the Great Spinner's plan. And we are all too busy to waste time questioning that.

I approached the offending leaf and looked it over. A birch, thrice my size. It had that odd flamboyant color that so many of the leaves were showing these recent years. The calm, lush green of the woods was giving way to new and garish pigments. And the leaves themselves were dryer, more brittle. Was that why prey was getting scarce? I'd have to ask some of the girls about that, after I was safely out from the open.

I cut away the ensnarled strands below while working in the drying leaf's shadow, making sure it wouldn't take my web down when it fell. Then I severed the silk holding the oddly bright leaf aloft, carefully keeping my eyes out for flying dangers. A gust of wind bounced me up and down on my handiwork, and I quickly spun an anchoring strand to the main stem of the web for insurance.

Life was too short to not learn from your mistakes.

One more cut, and the parched leaf was free, slowly drifting in lazy spirals down to the trail floor. I quickly repaired the large gash in the web the leaf had caused, eyes on the sky all the while.

Betty called out, "Giants!" the web ringing with her warning.

I froze, and then sprinted back under the cover of the still thickly green branch that was my home. I could feel the terrible, familiar tremors of the Giants that amble along the trail, dealing death as they rumbled by.

It had been at least 50 years ago, when I was still young. I wove quick but poorly designed webs then, priding myself on how much silk I could throw up in a year's time. Thelma was always more cautious, meticulously weaving small, tight webs. "Take your time, for goodness' sake," she warned me every year, it seemed.

I'd always reply, "You weave your web, and I'll weave mine." I was a bit of a bitch back then, I guess.

The Dark part of the year was coming. A Japanese beetle had blundered into my trap. They were hard-shelled and bitter, but nonetheless a meal. I was hungry and reckless, and dashed out on one of the frailer strands that splintered off from my web's main line. The thin silk slid along my hands, and I overshot the ensnared insect, just as it flapped its wings. Down I went and as I did, to my horror I felt the mammoth plodding of a Giant inexorably heading my way.

Thank the Great Spinner I had kept a safety line attached to the web. I caught myself halfway between web and earth, while the Ground below shook with each approaching Giant-step. As I frantically pulled myself up that one single string, I saw it clearly. A terrible phenomenon, big as a small tree, but moving steadily along the Ground.

What were these monsters? Were they primal forces, like the storm clouds above that drenched us with rain? I pulled myself up, up, back up to the hopeful safety of my web. The Giant stopped below me. I had never been so close to one before. Its scent, its color, all screamed that it was a living thing like we sisters, and the birds, and the prey we ate. But so huge, and oblivious...

I'd dashed past the forgotten beetle to the hidden sanctuary of my aerial home, shaken. For years, I'd warbled on the webs about my brush with the Giant. I guess the girls got a bit sick of my tale. None of them ever talked about venturing down to the Ground though.

This time, the Giant moved on without stopping. I could breathe again and thank the Great Spinner that I would survive. As the Giant's tremors receded, I noticed that more of the leaves around me were turning that odd, brilliant shade away from green. Perhaps next year, I'll be able to eat. And tell the sisters again about my brush with the Giant, and share the stories weaved after the Dark has passed.

ABOUT THE AUTHORS

James and Cheryl Maxey are frequently found at comic conventions and renaissance festivals selling Cheryl's crochet critters and James' books, including the *Bitterwood* saga, *Dragon Apocalypse*, and the *Dragonsgate* trilogy. With years of experience publishing and selling books, they decided to expand their publishing empire to include a diverse range of international authors writing high-quality science fiction and fantasy crafted for younger readers via Word Balloon Books.

Laurence Raphael Brothers is a writer and a technologist. He has published over 40 short stories in such magazines as *Nature*, *PodCastle*, and *Galaxy's Edge*. His noir urban fantasy novellas *The Demons of Wall Street*, *The Demons of the Square Mile*, and *The Demons of Chiyoda* are available from Mirror World Publishing. Pronouns: he/him.

Michael A. Clark's work has been published in *Galaxy's Edge*, *Liquid Imagination*, *Mystery Weekly Magazine*, *Gypsum Sound Tales* anthologies *Colp* and *Thuggish Itch*, *Tales from the Moonlit Path*, *Cosmic Horror Magazine*, the benefit anthology *Burning Love and Bleeding Hearts*, and *Moonlight & Misadventure*. His short story "Cold Surprise" was published in White Cat Publications. Clark lives in Charlotte, North Carolina and works in industrial automation while spending as much time as he can outdoors. He writes short stories and music because that's what he does. Baseball is Clark's sports addiction, and he proudly admits it.

R.C. Capasso has been composing stories since learning to read. After working in education, R. C. now devotes time to travel, learning languages, and reading and writing in a variety of genres. Previous short stories have appeared in *Literally Stories*, *Bewildering Stories*, *Zooscape* and *Fiction on the Web*, as well as online and print anthologies.

Eliza Wheaton is a seventh grader at Walter Reed Middle School and active in the, National Junior Honors Society, robotics club, and speech and debate. She is also a fencer, an avid reader, a committed environmentalist, and the companion of one betta fish, Francis, and one cat, Sarah. This is her first short story.

Mark Wheaton is a screenwriter (*Friday the 13th*, *The Messengers*, *Voice from the Stone*, etc.) and novelist (*Quake Cities*, *Fr. Chavez Trilogy*, *Emily Eternal*). His first horror short story, "In the Water," appeared in the 2021

About the Authors

Stoker Award-nominated anthology, *Worst Laid Plans*, from Grindhouse Press.

William Shaw is a writer from Sheffield, currently living in the USA. His writing has appeared in *Star*Line, Spaceports & Spidersilk,* and *Doctor Who Magazine.* His favourite fairy tale is, unsurprisingly, Jack and the Beanstalk.

Alex Shvartsman is the author of *The Middling Affliction* (2022) and *Eridani's Crown* (2019) fantasy novels. Over 120 of his stories have appeared in *Analog, Nature, Strange Horizons,* etc. He won the WSFA Small Press Award for Short Fiction (2014) and was a two-time finalist (2015 & 2017) for the Canopus Award for Excellence in Interstellar Fiction. His translations from Russian have appeared in *F&SF, Clarkesworld, Tor.com, Asimov's,* etc. Alex has edited over a dozen anthologies, including the long-running *Unidentified Funny Objects* series. He's the editor-in-chief of *Future Science Fiction Digest.* Alex resides in Brooklyn, NY. His website is www.alexshvartsman.com.

Sonja Thomas (she/her) writes stories for readers of all ages, often featuring brave, everyday girls doing extraordinary things. She's a contributing author for *Good Night Stories for Rebel Girls: 100 Real-Life Tales of Black Girl Magic.* Raised in Central Florida—home of the wonderful world of Disney, humidity, and hurricanes—and a Washington, DC transplant for eleven years (Go Nats!), she's now "keeping it weird" in the Pacific Northwest. *Sir Fig Newton and the Science of Persistence* is her debut novel.

Glenn Dungan is currently based in Brooklyn, NYC. He exists within a Venn-diagram of urban design, sociology, and good stories. When not obsessing about one of those three, he can be found at a park drinking black coffee and listening to podcasts about murder. For more of his work, see my website: whereisglennnow.com

Ian C Douglas is best known for his mid-grade science-fiction series 'The Zeke Hailey Adventures'. The books won the 2020 Eyelands Award and was shortlisted for the Gertrude Warner award 2021. He writes short stories, mostly in the speculative genre. His 'Haunting of the Jabberwocky' won the Gravity Award 2021. Ian mentors emerging writers, runs creative writing workshops and serves as a literacy ambassador. He graduated with an MA in Creative Writing (Distinction) and is a founder of the Nottingham Writers Studio. Ian appeared as guest-of-honor at Malta Festival of the Literary Stars in 2019.

Wendy Nikel is a speculative fiction author with a degree in elementary education, a fondness for road trips, and a terrible habit of forgetting where she's left her cup of tea. Her short fiction has been published by *Analog, Beneath Ceaseless Skies, Nature,* and elsewhere. Her time travel novella series, beginning with *The Continuum,* is available from World Weaver Press. For more info, visit wendynikel.com

Lena Ng roams the dimensions of Toronto, Canada, and is a monster-hunting member of the Horror Writers Association. She has curiosities published in seventy tomes including *Amazing Stories* and the anthology *We Shall Be Monsters,* which was a finalist for the 2019 Prix Aurora Award. *Under an Autumn Moon* is her short story collection.

Kay Hanifen was born on a Friday the 13th and once lived for three months in a haunted castle. Obviously, she had to become a horror writer. Her articles have appeared in *Ghouls Magazine* and *Screen Rant;* and her short stories have appeared in *Strangely Funny VIII, Crunchy with Ketchup, Dark Shadows: The Gay Nineties, Wicked Newsletters, Death of a Bad Neighbor, Enchanted Entrapments, Terror in the Trenches, Slice of Paradise,* and *Beware the Bugs.* When she's not consuming pop culture with the voraciousness of a vampire at a 24-hour blood bank, you can usually find her at kayhanifenauthor.wordpress.com.

Mark Cowling is a writer from Essex, UK. His work has been featured in BBC Radio sketchshows and many places online, such as *Daily Science Fiction* and *SFS Stories.* His short fiction was included in the 2021 anthology, *Campfire Macabre,* and was a winner of the 2020 Yahoo! Stor14s competition.

Janice Rider has always loved the natural world and resides in Calgary close to the Rocky Mountains. She has a BSc in Zoology with a minor in English Literature and a BEd degree with a science teaching specialty. Janice directs The Chameleon Drama Club for children and youth. Three of her plays for youth have been published through Eldridge Plays and Musicals. As well, a nonfiction piece of hers on snakes was accepted for publication last fall by *Honeyguide Literary Magazine.* And, yes, she once had the privilege of owning a millipede!

Kevin Hopson has dabbled in many genres over the years, but crime fiction and fantasy are his true loves. His novelette, *Pursuing the Dead,* was a 2019 Author Shout Reader Ready Awards winner. And if you're a fan of light fantasy, check out *The Emperor's Guard* series. You can learn more about Kevin by visiting his website at http://www.kmhopson.com.

About the Authors

Eileen Nunez is a New Jersey native who loves to read, write, and get completely absorbed in movies. She holds a Bachelors of Arts in Media and enjoys the magic of animation and moving making. For fun she reads ghost stories and all things paranormal. She has two self-published short stories and is currently working on a full-length novel. When not writing, she enjoys cuddles from her puppy Jarvis and taking walks in the park.

Evan Tong is a God-fearing man, a devoted husband, and father of two wonderful children. He experimented with fictional writing when visiting his parents, which allowed him not to cook every single meal for a brief period of time. He is a fitness and music enthusiast and enjoys playing the classical guitar while his daughter sings Taylor Swift songs.

Daniel R. Robichaud lives and writes in Humble, Texas. His fiction has been collected in *Hauntings & Happenstances: Autumn Stories* as well as *Gathered Flowers, Stones, and Bones: Fabulist Tales,* both from Twice Told Tales Press. He writes weekly reviews of film and fiction at the *Considering Stories* (https://consideringstories.wordpress.com/) website.

Peter Wood is an attorney in Raleigh, North Carolina, where he lives with his very patient wife. *Bull Spec* published Pete's first short story in 2010. Since then he has had over seventy stories published in *Asimov's, Stupefying Stories, Daily Science Fiction, Page and Spine Fiction Showcase* and *Every Day Fiction* and other markets. He wrote and assistant produced the film *Quantum Doughnut* in 2019 and is working on several podcasts. He grew up in Ottawa, Canada, but has lived in the South since 1988. He specializes in Southern Fried Science Fiction.

Sean Jones lives in Morrison Colorado and has worked on the Orion lunar capsule and the Dream Chaser spaceplane. Some of his science fiction is based on the *Hovercars* tabletop game, found on Amazon, while his swords & sorcery stories can be read in *Eldritch Science* and *Swords & Sorcery* online. His is an advocate of electric-assist bikes and a modernizer of elderly vehicles.

Rufa Formica is a brobdingnagian, radioactive, psychokinetic ant created to destroy mankind. His hobbies are picnicking, digging tunnels, and crushing his enemies.